THE SEAL'S TEMPTATION

WOUNDED HEARTS- BOOK 7

JACQUIE BIGGAR

WAVEFRONT PUBLISHING

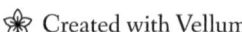

INTRODUCTION

DEA agent Maggie Holt has been through hell and back.

After eighteen months undercover in a Mexican cartel, Maggie is broken. The kickass agent she once was, is gone, leaving her riddled with guilt and nightmares. Forced to take paid leave, Maggie accepts the offer of a vacation on the ranch of the man who'd rescued her from an almost certain death.

Frank Stein knows the signs of PTSD, he's suffered the symptoms himself as Chief Petty Officer of SEAL Team Five. Honorably discharged from duty, Frank has found peace at the family ranch and hopes it will do the same for Magdalena. Ever since he'd first met her when she was interrogating his buddy, Jared, Frank has been fascinated by the raven-haired beauty and wants the chance to see where their relationship could go.

Adam O'Connor is Maggie's partner. He knows her. He loved her once and could again, if she'd let him in. But he's also angry she took the chances she did by going undercover against orders. And now, things are different. She's different.

When a right-wing militia group infiltrates the area, will DEA Agent Maggie Holt, her partner, Adam O'Connor, and ex-SEAL Chief Frank Stein be able to set aside their differences to stop them before someone dies? And who will Maggie choose, the handsome cowboy, or her charismatic DEA partner?

PRAISE FOR JACQUIE BIGGAR

"Those of you who love military romance, wounded warrior romance and romantic suspense will love the stories written by this super talented, fabulous author!"

— TAMMY

"Jacquie Biggar had me reading romantic suspense well past my bedtime. The characters are so well written they could walk right off the page!"

— AVONNA- THE ROMANCE REVIEWS

"Jacquie Biggar has a wonderful gift for writing hot and extremely likable military men!"

— JACQUI NELSON

"This author is an auto-buy for me. Each of her novels including this one is a perfect mix of angst, suspense, humor, and steaminess."

— STEPHANIE

For my extended Family, the readers who have fallen in love with the Wounded Hearts series as much as I have.

Jacquie

1

Frank Stein sat at the scarred wooden dinner table that had graced his family home since long before he was born. The combined aromas of roasted turkey, sage stuffing, garlic mashed potatoes and poultry gravy had his mouth watering and stomach growling. No one cooked better than his momma.

On his right, best friend, Jared Martin and wife Annie, visited with Frank's mother, Emily, and her new beau, Spencer, while Adam and his boss bickered in the background, but it was the silent woman on his left that commanded his attention.

Magdalena Holt.

His fascination with the mysterious DEA agent had grown almost embarrassingly obvious to everyone, it seemed, except her. She was too focused on stopping an international human trafficking ring to worry about his tender feelings.

Emily's black lab, Sugar, lounged on the floor at Maggie's feet, as though he sensed her underlying torment. Every now and then, Frank caught her sneaking a piece of meat to the dog, but he pretended not to notice. She could give the animal the whole damn bird if it made her feel better.

Her recent abduction left him angry and helpless. The vibrant, commanding agent he'd met months ago, when Jared called from Las Vegas asking for help, was nowhere to be seen in the timid, pale imitation sitting at a table full of laughing, chattering friends.

The dark place in his head wanted to reach out and shake her silly. How could she have allowed herself to be placed in danger that way? At the same time, his arms ached from the restraint he placed on himself not to grab hold and never let go. He'd gladly protect her with his life.

But, that was the problem; she didn't need him. She never had.

And to prove his point...

"Hey, Mags, any word on the girl you saved from that crash?" Her partner, Adam, turned his mega-watt smile her way and grasped the fingers fiddling with her fork instead of eating.

"Hmm?" she murmured, the low hum sending vibrations through Frank's gut, and lower. "Molly? No, but the hospital promised to keep me informed." She gave a faint smile. "Thanks for helping her parents with the repatriation order.

I was worried she'd have to remain in Mexico over Easter until trial was set."

He gave her a warm hug, his blond hair a stark contrast to the inky darkness of Maggie's. Frank wanted to rip them apart. Not a good reaction for a SEAL Chief, even if he was retired. He had no right to feel jealous. Maggie had never shown any sign of interest—it was all wishful thinking on his part. Which was ridiculous. He was a thirty-seven-year-old war veteran acting like a kid wet behind the ears with his first crush.

He turned to Jared, determined to give the agents some privacy. "How big is that son of yours getting to be, Martin? Good thing he takes after his mom and doesn't have to carry your ugly puss on his shoulders for the rest of his life."

"Frank," his mother chided.

Jared just laughed. "I agree, buddy." He tugged Annie close for a kiss that left her cheeks glowing. "I hit the jackpot with this one."

Adam snorted. "No more gambling for you, remember?"

Annie's smile was soft. "Don't worry, he doesn't have to wager a thing on me. I'm a sure bet when it comes to my husband."

Jared kissed her again. "How did I get so damn lucky?"

Frank was happy for his friend. Jared had gone through a rough patch after Adam took a hit in the teams and died—or so they'd thought. Now he was a husband and father with a fledgling security business and Adam was a DEA agent with a distractingly sexy partner.

Times, they do change.

Maggie set her napkin on the table and pushed her chair back, disturbing Sugar's nap. "Excuse me," she muttered. Her gaze flitted around the room. "I just... need some air."

"Of course, honey," Emily said, her expression concerned. "Frank will go with you."

Maggie's gaze jumped to him and away again. "Oh, no, that's okay. Enjoy your dinner. I'm fine."

Translation; *leave me alone.*

Frank gave Sugar the signal and the dog glided behind Maggie as she opened the screen and stepped out the door.

Adam started to rise at the same time Frank did but sank into his seat with a slight nod. "Thanks, Chief."

There was nothing to thank him for, he would have followed her without his mother's meddling.

The porch was cool after the warmth of the house, reminding him that summer was still a promise on the horizon. He found her sitting on his momma's swing, still as a shadow.

He leaned on the rail a few feet away, suddenly feeling like a bull in a china shop. "Sorry about the racket in there. The boys and I haven't seen each other in a while."

She leaned forward, the chains holding the chair to the rafters creaking, and rubbed Sugar behind the ear. "No, it was nice—listening to you joking like that. I can tell you're close."

His lips quirked. That was one way of putting it. "Yes, ma'am, I guess we are. They're my brothers."

The swing slowed its rocking motion. "You mean the SEAL Team. The one Adam belonged to?"

He nodded and stared at the explosion of stars in the evening sky—and thought about another night when the explosions weren't nearly as peaceful. "Most of us were together straight out of BUD/S training—'cept Nick and his MWD, Jake. Remember them?" *Of course she does, you idiot. It's thanks to you that she ended up on the cartel's shit list.*

"Yes," she said so softly he had to lean in to hear her. "Tidal Falls, right?" She shivered and rattled the chains above her head.

Damn, he needed to get that oiled. If it bothered him, she must be about ready to climb the walls. She didn't seem upset though, just... sad.

He straightened and took the two strides necessary to reach the throw lying across the back of one of the rocking chairs set up to look out over the ranch compound. He shook it out to make sure no creepy crawlies had set up house and handed it across the distance.

"Here, take this. Unless you'd prefer—"

"No," she said, a little too forcefully. She backed it up with a nervous laugh as she wrapped the blanket around her shoulders. "Sorry, your family has been great, truly. It's just a bit much yet, after... well, everything." She set the swing rocking again with short little jabs of her toe. "Tell me about... BUD/S, was it?"

She reminded him of a wall clock he'd taken apart one time as a kid, curious to see how it all worked. The outside was smooth, seemingly unbreakable, but once he'd undone the screws at the back and fiddled around a bit, springs popped and the whole thing fell apart.

Frank was determined not to let that happen to Magdalena Holt.

"Sure, whatever you want," he said, aware there were things he could never talk about of his time in the Teams. "BUD/S stands for Basic Underwater Demolition SEAL School, but there's nothing basic about it. It's twenty-four weeks of grueling physical and mental training. But then, you DEA agents probably go through some pretty rigorous stuff yourselves."

She smiled, just a flash of white really, but it was enough to suffuse his chest with warmth. And, make him wish for better lighting out here so he could see her expressions.

"Nice non-answer, Chief."

He shook his head. "Just Frank, ma'am. I haven't been Chief for a while now."

"Do you miss it?" she asked, her head tipping to the side as though she really cared to hear what he had to say.

Wishful thinking.

"Sure," he acknowledged. "It was a big part of my life for

a decade—more, counting training—but it was time to move on, let the next crew take up the sword. I'd lost the drive and that could get my men killed. It was time."

They looked out over the valley with the brook bubbling away in the distance, cows lowing contentedly, and lights twinkling from the homes of the ranch staff. A rare sense of peace fell over him. He could easily see himself sitting in these old rocking chairs twenty years from now with Maggie at his side. Damn, he had it bad.

"Yeah," she whispered. "It's time."

2

A dam smiled and said all the right things—he hoped—but his attention was on the two silhouettes visible through the kitchen window. Frank's broad outline was easy to identify as he leaned against the railing a few feet away from the porch swing Mags had claimed. At least she wasn't alone out there, though he wished...

"Penny for your thoughts?" Amanda asked, intelligent green eyes not missing a thing.

SAC Amanda Rhinehold had won his respect during the Mexico op to rescue Maggie. She'd greased wheels and gained them official entry into the country in time to save his partner from certain death.

He decided to settle with a half-truth. "I'm worried about Mags. She's... different."

Amanda raised a brow. "What did you expect, O'Connor? She spent the last few months trying to stay alive while being tortured by a depraved monster. It's not something you get over—ever."

Adam's gut tightened. If Chenglei weren't already dead, he'd kill him himself—slowly and painfully.

"Anything I can do to help?" Jared asked from across the food-laden table. "I owe Agent Holt for saving my ass—sorry ma'am," he said, glancing to the head of the table where Frank's mom sat, "—butt, in Vegas."

"No apology needed. Believe me, in forty-odd years of ranching I've heard worse." Emily smiled, her quicksilver eyes—so like her son's—crinkling at the corners. She turned to Amanda. "As that young woman's commanding officer, I assume you have the means to insist on a period of recuperation. Frank and I would be happy to have her stay on for a spell. This land heals the deepest aches. Believe me, I know."

Spencer grasped her hand and she regarded him gratefully. "I lost my husband, and then later, my youngest son, and there was a time I thought I'd lose Frank, too. My home is the only thing I had to hang onto, and... it helped. Now look—" she waved her free hand around the table, "—you all are here, and my heart is overflowing." She put a fist to her chest and blinked away tears.

Annie's eyes welled up. "I know just how you feel, Mrs. Stein. When Jared left to join the Navy, I thought my world was over, but his mom welcomed me and my baby into her home and I'll be forever grateful. The ranch would be good for Maggie—if she'll stay."

Everyone turned their gaze on Adam.

"Don't look at me, Maggie does her own thing. Why do you think she ended up in that hellhole?" He rubbed a frustrated hand behind his neck. "I specifically told her to wait for backup. She was determined to bring that ring down single-handed and almost paid with her life."

"Get over yourself, O'Connor." Amanda calmly took a drink of the hair-raising coffee Spencer had brewed. "Agent Holt knew what she was getting into. She came to me and expressed her resolve to go undercover. I cleared her for the investigation. *Me*." She stared at him—unblinking—over the rim of the cup. "You're both DEA agents, Adam. It's what you do. Stop blaming yourself and concentrate on closing this case. We still have a long way to go." She set the cup down and pushed her chair back in the sudden silence. "Pardon me, it's been a lengthy day. I think I'm going to call it a night."

Adam rose as well, unwilling to give her the last word. "I'll show you to your room. Thank you for a delicious meal, Mrs. Stein. Jared, see you in the morning?"

"Of course. Frank promised us a trail ride—if you can handle it, *Ace*?"

Adam smiled at his old call sign. "Can't say there's many chances to get on a horse in Vegas, but sure, I'll be there."

He waited for Amanda to navigate the mish-mash of

chairs circling the farmhouse table, then followed her into the narrow hall. "It's this way," he said, directing her past a large den filled with dark, heavy-looking furniture, an office he remembered from previous visits, a washroom, complete with clawfoot tub and shower, and finally the two rooms allotted to them at the back of the home.

Amanda reached for her door handle. "Well, goodnight," she murmured, seemingly awkward now they were alone.

It was like she wore a mask in public and only let it drop when he caught her off guard. He liked her better without the professional façade.

"Wait." He grasped her wrist and felt a quiver. Was she afraid of him? She had to know he'd never hurt a woman—it went against everything he stood for as an officer of the law, and a man.

He let her go and leaned against the opposite wall to give her space. "I wanted to talk to you before we turn in. Got a sec?"

She sighed, the sweep of nut-brown hair on her forehead lifting with her breath. "Yeah, of course. I'm not going to apologize for what I said, though. You've wallowed in guilt for long enough, it's affecting your performance on the job. It's my duty to assess your ability to set aside personal problems. If I don't feel you're up to the task, I *will* pull you from duty. Do you understand, Agent O'Connor?"

Adam frowned, all thoughts of how pretty she looked against the eggshell beadboard and soft lighting squashed under a growing resentment. "And here I was thinking you liked me," he quipped.

She had the grace to look embarrassed. At least that was something in his favor.

"I *do* like you, Adam. Maybe too much, which is why I need to set boundaries." She waved a hand between them and lifted her chin.

She looked more like a spitting kitten in the flowing white dress she'd chosen for dinner, than the stiff poker-up-her-butt image she portrayed at the office. He knew which one he preferred.

He traced a finger over the tiny crescent-shaped scar decorating her lip. "What happened?" he asked, sensing it was an important piece of the woman she'd become.

Her eyes dilated at his touch. She brushed his hand away and licked at the spot with the tip of her tongue, sending a jolt of awareness to his groin.

"It was a long time ago. I try not to think about it," she said, her voice little more than a whisper. "It's late, I should—"

"Thank you," he interrupted, unwilling to let her go. Once he closed the door to his room, he'd be alone with his demons and he wasn't ready for that yet.

She tipped her head and the lush thickness of her hair fell over her shoulder. "For what?"

"Hmm?" he murmured, distracted by the rich curls cupping her breast. "Oh, for saying what you said back there

—in the kitchen." He met her gaze. "You're right. I've been blaming myself for months now—years really, if you count the subterfuge with the Team—and it's getting to where I can't stand my own company. I needed someone I respect to set me in my place. Quit wallowing, is how I think you put it?" He smiled to let her know he didn't take offense.

She slowly returned his smile, the upward curve of her lips tempting him to go places he knew were out of bounds.

"You don't strike me as the wallowing type, O'Connor." She slipped through the door to her bedroom. Her eyes glowed with mischief. "Goodnight, Adam," she said as she closed the door.

"See you in the morning, Amanda."

He stood there for a long time after, grinning foolishly.

3

Maggie stared at the evening sky, fingers clenching and unclenching in the folds of the blanket around her shoulders. She was almost preternaturally aware of the man sitting like a silent guardian in the too-small rocker a few feet away.

Desperate to break what felt like an awkward silence, she gestured toward the sparkling constellations over their heads. "Do you study the stars, Mr. Stein? You have quite the view out here." Maybe not as reach-out-and-touch them as she'd felt on that mesa in Mexico, but a hell of a lot safer. The melancholy that was never very far away filled her chest, a black cloud covering the silvery moon. Her best friend was buried on that hill, a victim of the monster who'd ruined the lives of countless women.

"Not really. My brother and I got into it some as kids but then he... disappeared and I kind of lost heart." Frank's voice flowed over her like a warm breeze, dispersing the darkness of her thoughts.

"I'm so sorry," she murmured. "I think I remember reading something about that in your file—the part that wasn't confidential anyway." She smiled.

He nodded. "It happened a long time ago. We've accepted it, though that's not to say we've stopped looking. Hope lives on, you know?"

Yeah, she did.

The only thing that kept her alive through those hellish months with Chenglei and his band of assholes was hope.

Well, that and a craving for revenge.

"I imagine you've exhausted official channels. Have you looked into private investigators?"

He shifted, stretching long jean-clad legs and crossing his ankles, revealing scuffed cowboy boots. The old chair creaked, protesting his movements.

"We tried every avenue there was, but it did no good. He'd vanished." Frank's voice was matter-of-fact, but his tone revealed how much the loss of his brother still affected him.

The sad truth was there were thousands just like Cameron Stein—young men and women dissatisfied with their lives who thought the grass would be greener on the other side and instead learned, more often than not and sometimes with fatal consequences, that running away was not the answer.

There probably wasn't a lot she could do, but Maggie wanted to help this family to at least find some closure. Maybe she could pull a few strings within the agency and see what popped. Off the record, of course.

She glanced through the window into the soft vignette-like lighting of the kitchen. Frank's mom had risen to clear the table, her hands grasping the platter of decimated turkey as she laughed at something the ranch foreman said, affection apparent on both their faces. Emily leaned down to give him a kiss and he took advantage of the moment to pull her onto his lap. Maggie looked away, her heart pinching.

That kind of relationship was as far away as the moon for her. Even before her captivity, Maggie's main focus had been career-oriented. Adam blamed himself for their break-up, but truthfully, she just wasn't a good bet.

"I'm not promising anything, but I'll check a couple of things when I get back to work. Sometimes, time can uncover secrets from the past." She didn't expect him to jump up and down with joy, but the non-reaction came as a bit of a surprise.

The side of his face, bathed in the light streaming through the window, was cast in a grim expression she couldn't understand. It should have made her nervous—that look—but on Frank it made her want to delve deeper. He was unlike any man she'd ever known; a mix of stoic and kind, strong and gentle, craggy and stalwart. He reminded her of the Texas hills he called home; protective and mysterious.

"Thanks," he answered. "It's just..."

"What?" she huffed, already regretting the impulse to butt her nose in where it didn't belong. *You'd think I'd learn.*

He stood and paced the porch from one end of the house to the other, the boards creaking beneath his boots. When he returned, she rose, her body tensing into a fight-or-flight she couldn't control. Sweat broke out across her forehead and under her arms and her ears thumped with her out of control pulse. She hated Chenglei for what he'd done to her.

Frank must have caught wind of her fear. He stopped in a bright patch of light, hands out at his sides—still as one of the Bur Oaks that dotted the countryside.

"I... I'm sorry," she whispered, angry and ashamed.

"Don't be," he said, his voice low and calm as though he were breaking a mustang.

Maybe he was. She felt half wild. Unable to slide out of the mindset of a victim, even though she'd been the predator —taking Chenglei's life without regret.

"I should leave." She unclenched her hands and felt the blood flow into her fingers. "This is a mistake."

Frank nodded and her stomach catapulted to her toes. A shameful part of her wished he would fight to keep her here, and how sad was that?

"Sure, whatever you need," he murmured. "But you might want to think it over. It's quiet here. No one to push you into doing anything before you're ready." He slowly, carefully took her hand, his fingers hard and calloused. "Don't rush away, Maggie. You'll only hurt someone if you do, and I don't think you want that. I've been in your shoes. PTSD is a bitch, make no mistake. It creeps up on you when you least expect it and tangles with your head. Do you really want to be in charge of a weapon when that happens?"

Well, when he put it that way.

She couldn't live with herself if another innocent died on her watch.

She tugged her fingers free and shoved her hands deep into her pockets. "I'll stay."

4

———

Dawn was little more than a blush on the horizon when Frank, Jared and Adam set out on their ride the next morning. It was both strange and bittersweet to have his friends on his six again. Frank grinned, the tension easing from between his shoulder blades. Just like old times.

He kicked Sadie into a fast trot and glanced over his shoulder. "You girls think you can keep up?"

Jared shot him a one finger salute. "Maybe if you'd given me a horse instead of this old nag." The *nag* in question—a handsome Quarter Horse Frank had trained himself—tossed his head, fighting the tight grip on the reins.

Adam leaned over and gave the bay a slap on the rump with his Red Sox ball cap, a rare smile erasing the grim lines of his face. "What's the matter, Martin? Married life turning you into a pansy?" He took one glance at his buddy's expression as he wrestled to bring the startled horse under control and decided to catch up to Frank. "Be one with the horse," he advised with a laugh.

"I knew you were an a-hole," Jared shouted.

Frank shook his head at their antics. "You two are worse than a couple of kids." He kept an eye on Jared until he caught up, then guided Sadie toward the hills, turning up the collar on his shearling jacket against the early morning chill.

Spencer stepped out the door of the foreman's cottage as they rode by and doffed his stained cowboy hat. "Have a good ride," he called.

Frank tipped his Stetson in reply but kept going. Spence had managed this ranch for upwards of thirty years—he didn't need Frank telling him what to do.

"He doesn't spend the night up at the main house?" Jared asked, his butt bouncing in the saddle.

"No, he does *not* sleep with my mother." Tempted to let him suffer, Frank warned, "Loosen your back. Roll with the motion and it'll go easier on you."

Adam whistled through his teeth. "I'm sensing some tension, Chief. You do realize your mother is a grown woman, right?" His puppy-dog eyes twinkled with mirth.

Frank snorted. "If you yahoos are done, can we get back to business?"

"Ah," Jared said, his teeth clacking together with every bounce. "I figured there had to be an ulterior motive to this invite."

Frank frowned. It was true he'd asked his friends to join them at the ranch after their return from Mexico, but he didn't mean for it to come with a price tag.

"Listen—" he began.

Jared held up a leather-gloved hand, then just as quickly latched onto the pommel as the bay climbed a steep rise. "Hey, it's all good. Annie and I have been meaning to come down for a visit anyway. Things have been slightly crazy back home, what with the new baby and setting up the new business and all, or we would have been here sooner." He gave Adam the stink-eye. "Especially, if you'd let me know you were in trouble."

Adam shrugged. "Don't look at me, bro, I was following orders. Besides, we had to move fast once we knew where that bastard had Mags."

They topped the rise and stopped for a moment to take in the vista. Cows grazed in the field below, their sleek brown and white coats a contrast to the verdant green grass. Bluebonnets flirted with the breeze blowing down from the north, keeping the temperature balmy—at least for the moment. Fluffy Cumulous clouds scattered across the sky like the petticoats under a woman's skirt; not that many wore them these days except for weddings and such. And why the heck was he thinking about a woman's underdrawers anyway? Frank scowled.

"Something wrong, Chief?" Adam looked from him to the field and back again. "Still having poacher problems?"

Frank nodded, happy to set aside his personal thoughts. "That's part of the reason for today's ride," he admitted. "Spencer's been looking into the numbers, and truthfully, it's not good. We've lost close to a hundred head, but that's not the worst of it. Someone is deliberately killing our calves."

Jared and Adam shared a glance.

"Am I missing something?" Jared asked. "Isn't it the calves that are worth the big bucks? Why would anyone just shoot them—I assume that's how they're dying?"

Frank jabbed a finger to a spot on the horizon. "There's something I want to show you."

"Lead the way," Adam said, his gaze sharpening.

Frank took a roundabout way of dropping into the field, following a well-worn game trail cutting its way down the hill. He was encouraged to see the cattle watching their progress before returning to their feed. At least they weren't spooked—today anyway.

An hour later they came up on the eastern boundary of the property. A paved road separated his land from their neighbors, the Finchs'. Another family with deep roots embedded in the Texas soil. He rode toward the barbed wire fence, his gut tightening with every stride.

"You mean to tell me we could have driven ourselves over here instead of getting out innards bounced around?" Jared lamented.

"Quit your whining, Martin. You're getting soft up there in Tidal Falls." Adam rode up beside Frank, eyes narrowing as he took in the speed limit sign leaning precariously over the road. "Wow, someone took offence to the posted limit," he murmured.

"That's one way of putting it," Frank agreed. The sun shone through at least a dozen holes pock-marking the rectangular white aluminum with its fifty mile an hour posting. He'd searched the base and area surrounding it the first time he came across the destruction, but whoever it was had been careful to cover their tracks. He hadn't been able to find even one bullet casing.

"Kids out for a joyride?" Jared asked, carefully dismounting. He hung onto the saddle for a minute, his face scrunched up in a grimace, then stepped away to stretch his legs and rub his butt. "Man, I'll take my truck any day over this abuse." The horse turned its head and chomped on the bit, big brown eyes seeming to silently laugh at his predicament. "It's not funny, horse. I think you did that on purpose."

"I'd be tempted to agree with you—about the sign, anyway—except this isn't a one-time thing and it's happening to my calves as well." Frank took his hat off and rubbed a hand through sweat-dampened hair. The sun was packing a punch today.

"Your calves? Why didn't you say something before?" Jared said, gazing at the animals peacefully grazing in the distance. "How many?"

"This year?" Frank answered, his tone unintentionally terse. "Ten, so far. Add that to the twelve from last year and we have a problem. Each animal is worth upwards of a thousand dollars when ready for market." He nodded to the drunken sign. "It's not just the one sign, either. Our neighbor across the road has had her chickens shot at. Another one had the tires blown out of his ranch truck and someone ransacked a line shack bordering our properties. Then there's the animal carcasses laid out alongside the road like a big *fuck you* to everyone who lives here. Deer, rabbits, owls, even a couple of coyotes. Most left to rot in the ditch with their guts eviscerated. These are sick assholes and I want them caught before they up the ante and take aim at one of us."

"Shit, Chief, I didn't realize it was this bad. The local Feds doing anything to help?" Adam's blue eyes glittered under the ball cap he'd lowered over his brow.

Frank avoided an immediate answer. He dismounted and led Sadie to a tall patch of grass before loosening her girth and tying the reins to the fence. Then he unlatched his saddlebag to remove a thermos of coffee before patting her flank, breathing in dust and horse. "Thanks for the safe ride, Sadie-girl."

He strode to where Adam and Jared were taking a closer look at the sign post. "Coffee?"

Jared turned and accepted a tin cup. "You're speaking my language." He inhaled over the steaming cup and sighed. "This, I needed." He raised his cup in a toast. "I am never out of the fight."

Frank straightened at the words—part of the SEAL

Ethos. Pride in these men he called brothers swelled his chest and locked his throat with emotion. They may have left the teams, but the navy still ran thick in their blood.

"Hooyah," he said, and Adam repeated the chant.

He looked out over the land that generations of Steins had called home. The rolling hills and valleys. The sun that could bake the soil dry or provide bountiful harvests. The stream that fed the pastures, and the cattle that keep the ranch alive, and he knew there was nothing he wouldn't do to protect what was his.

Nothing.

5

Brian Finch wiped his mouth and threw the soiled napkin on his plate. His new friends were still working through their meals, shoulders hunched over the food like pigs at a trough. They reminded him of gluttons, forking piles of grub in like there was no tomorrow. If it wasn't for the cash they'd promised him when the job was done, he'd cut them loose. But he needed the money. It was his ticket out of this hellhole.

He glanced at his father's grim, bruised face and guilt soured his stomach. "I thought I told you to leave my parents alone."

The one on the right looked up and, as usual, his oddly colored eyes, one brown, one blue, sent an icy shiver down Brian's spine. "Then he'd better learn to keep out of our way. We ain't here to molly-coddle no old-timers." He smacked his companion's arm and they both snickered. "You made us a deal, remember?"

A deal with the devil, more like. While these two reminded him of bullies in a schoolyard, their boss put the *E* in evil. Brian still couldn't believe he'd been the guy's cell mate. Five long years. Half the time he'd expected a shiv in the gut, and the rest was spent owned by a man without remorse.

A man who taught Brian to hate.

And now he was beholden to the bastard.

But soon his debts would be paid, and he'd be free to do whatever the hell he wanted. One job. He could keep his shit together that long—he had to.

"I was in town today. There's talk of a renegade group of vandals destroying property, killing livestock, and shooting at vehicles." He pinned Lennox of the strange eyes, and Jenkins, all brawn and little brain, with a steely gaze. "I know you aren't that fricking stupid. Draw attention to us and your asses are on the line. I won't take the rap. If Rivero hears..."

"Who's gonna tell him?" Lennox snarled. "Just do what you're supposed to, kid, and mind your own business."

Brian shoved back his chair, fists clenched, but a wheezing cough from behind him stilled his hands. He turned as his mom shuffled into the room, eyes red and watery.

"Ma, you should be in bed," he scolded, taking her elbow to guide her to his chair. He sent a warning glare at Lennox and Jenkins. "Sit down, these two were just on their way out."

Jenkins shoved another dinner roll in his mouth, and rose, kicking the leg of Lennox's chair. "C'mon, man, I need a beer."

Brian's dad snorted, earning a scowl from Lennox. "Got something to say, old man?"

"You guys better hurry up. It's an hour to town and the bar closes at eleven weeknights." Brian folded his arms over his too-thin chest and waited. He might have been a nothing in jail, but out here he was his own man and he wasn't going to take any crap from a couple of idiots.

Jenkins grinned, revealing a silver-plated tooth. "You like to play with fire, kid, I'll give you that."

He threw the half-eaten bun on the table and Brian watched it wobble like a decapitated head. He swallowed the bile rising up his gorge and forced an answering smirk. "Whatever lets you sleep at night, buddy. Just remember what I said." Rivero had made him boss, they'd better get used to it.

"Don't wait up, Pops. We're not so light on our feet after a few beers, wouldn't want you to have an... accident." Lennox winked as he and Jenkins ambled out the door in their Hawaiian shirts, leaving a strained silence in their wake.

Momma rose and began to clear the table, her hands shaking so bad the dishes rattled.

"Put them down, for Pete's sake, before you break something," Brian's dad growled. He rose, winced, and hobbled to the door. Holding his ribs, he slid the curtain to the side, peered out the dark window, then snapped the deadbolt home. "I'm calling the sheriff."

"No," Brian barked. He took the plates from his mom and carried them to the sink, before turning to face his dad. "Do you really want me back in prison that bad?"

"Of course, he doesn't," Momma cried, following to reach up and pat his cheeks. "Your father, he worries about you, *niño*."

Brian grasped her hands and placed a gentle kiss on their calloused palms. "And I'm worried about *you*. I've been promised a lot of money, Momma. Enough to get you the best doctors and pay for the treatments they prescribe—whatever it takes."

He turned to his old man. Unwilling sympathy rose. He looked... beaten down. For so many years, Brian had nurtured a grudge against the man who'd let him go to jail without even offering assistance. But now, now he just wanted to help his family and then get the hell out of Dodge. There was a big old world out there and by damn, he was going to see it.

"C'mon, Dad. A couple of weeks at most and we'll be out of your hair. You can put up with us for that long, can't you?"

His father's gaze took in his wife of forty years and the son who'd caused them heartache. "Help your mother with the dishes," he said, then slowly made his way out of the room. A minute later, Brian heard the bedroom door creak shut.

He sighed. "He's never going to forgive me, is he?"

Momma leaned on the counter as though it could hold her up and wiped her damp forehead. "It's tough for him. He has his pride. Those men, they are not good. Your father knows this. Just as he knows he is not as strong as he used to be." She grasped Brian's arm when he would have turned away. "Give him time, *niño*, he will come around."

Brian smiled to offer her peace of mind, but inside he wondered how he was going to gain time when it felt as though the hourglass was running dry.

6

M aggie was awake when the men rode out of the yard, their figures tall and straight in the saddle. Even though dawn hadn't grabbed hold of the day yet, it was easy to distinguish between the three. Adam rode in the middle, the Zen to Frank and Jarrod's more gregarious personalities—though he didn't mind instigating a ruckus now and then. She grinned as he swept off his beat up old Red Sox cap and slapped Jarrod's horse on the rear causing it to dance sideways.

Her gaze migrated to Frank, his shoulders wide enough to carry the weight of the world, but she sensed he was exhausted. She could only imagine the danger his duties had entailed as a Navy SEAL along with the stress of losing his father and brother. He was a strong man. One who instilled undying loyalty in his men. Did he realize how rare that sort of connection was?

She let the curtain fall on their departure and turned toward the door, suddenly eager to escape her demons. The hallway was dark and silent, the other guests taking advantage of the comfortable beds and homemade blankets to get a little extra snuggle time. Maggie envied them. The nightmares of her time as Chenglei's slave were so vivid she often woke in a cold sweat, her hand reaching for the nearest weapon. She'd gone undercover to ruin him, but she was the one who'd been destroyed.

"Oh, hello, dear," Frank's mom said as Maggie entered the kitchen, hoping for a cup of coffee before the house came alive. Mrs. Stein smiled from her spot in front of the stove, a spatula in hand. "I was just getting the pancakes going. I hope you're hungry." She pointed the kitchen tool toward a coffee-maker sitting by the sink. "Coffee's there. Frank bought me one of those new-fangled single pod machines, it took a while to get used to it after using a percolator for so many years." She chuckled.

Maggie smiled and made her way across the spacious kitchen to the machine. Soon the aroma of dark roast coffee wafted into the room and she closed her eyes in bliss. She'd never take such a simple pleasure for granted again.

Turning, filled cup in hand, she raised it slightly. "Need one?" she asked her hostess.

Mrs. Stein nodded. "That would be lovely, thank you." She waited until Maggie set the mug on the counter to ask, "Did you get a good rest? Frank put you up in his old room as it's at the back of the house away from the racket." She expertly flipped a plate-sized pancake, then gave Maggie a commiserating glance. "He's worried about you, we all are."

Maggie stared at her, startled. The woman barely knew her. And even worse, her son had risked his life to rescue Maggie from a Mexican drug lord. She should hate her, instead of welcoming Maggie into the Stein home. Maggie didn't know what to do with her kindness, so she veered away from it. "Mind if I take my coffee out to the porch?"

Mrs. Stein gave her a kind look mixed with sadness and nodded. "Of course. I'll call when the others are up." She lifted the frisbee-sized pancake out of the pan and added it to the pile already resting in the warming oven, before pouring more batter in the sizzling pan.

Knowing she'd disappointed the woman, but unable to breach the distance she'd created, Maggie took her sorry self out the door. The air was brisk this early and served to snap her out of the funk she'd fallen into. It was easy to see why Frank loved the land so much. It seemed... endless. To a girl who'd grown up under the lights of the Vegas strip, this place was another world.

She wandered over to the railing and leaned against the whitewashed wood, sipping her coffee with a deep sigh of appreciation. At some point she was going to have to make decisions about her life, but for now, she was content to just float along and try not to think. Her mother used to say running wasn't the answer, but standing strong hadn't done her much good, either.

Gradually she became aware of the creek gurgling as it wound along the south side of the homestead, a log cabin squatting on its bank. Songbirds welcomed the morning, while far off, a rooster woke the hens. A fine mist rose off the grass creating rainbow prisms in the air. Down the hill, a giant two-story barn stood, its doors propped open with hay bales. A moment later, the ranch foreman, Spencer Tate, appeared in the opening leading a spirited gray horse with black mane and tail. Maggie stood, transfixed. The stallion towered over the man, leashed power in the arch of his proud neck and dancing hooves. His ears flickered and he stilled, seeming to look right at her.

"Ghost," Maggie murmured, her heart taking flight in her breast. As a child she'd dreamed of a horse like this one. An animal who'd protected her from her father's angry fists. But, of course, it vanished when her eyes opened and the pain took over.

"There you are."

Annie Martin's cheerful voice yanked her out of the past. She shuddered, tearing her gaze away from the horse as it was led to an enclosed paddock. "Here I am," she agreed, lifting her cup in a mocking salute. The other woman looked way too chirpy with her curly auburn locks and freckled cheeks.

Friendly green eyes seemed to size up her attitude and

shrug it off with a smile. "Isn't this place great? I've been trying to get Jared to bring me here forever, but with the wedding and the baby, not to mention the restaurant... sorry, I tend to get carried away. You'll get used to me." She grinned and turned as Agent Rhinehold stepped out the door. "Good morning."

Amanda Rhinehold quirked a delicate brow. "Have a good sleep?"

"You bet. No little gremlins waking us up at oh-dark-hundred, it was wonderful." Annie laughed and took a sip from her still steaming mug.

Maggie looked on, a little envious—for the coffee—not the kids. Or so she told herself. "How old are they? Two boys, right?" See, she could ask normal everyday questions like a normal everyday person—go her.

Annie's face lit up as she set her cup down and dug into the knapsack she carried over one shoulder. Diapers, wipes, bandages, the kitchen sink, she had everything and then some in there. A moment later, she tugged a ragged leather wallet from the pouch and opened it to reveal, yep, family photos. Maggie caught Rhinehold's grimace and smirked. At least she wasn't in baby purgatory alone.

"Look, aren't they adorable?" Annie said, holding up a string of pictures like you might get from one of those photo booths at a fair. A tall boy with Annie's hair and Jared's eyes stood next to a chubby baby sitting on a stool, maybe five or six months old. He was grinning and waving a teddy bear at whoever took the pictures. It was one of those photos parents kept to show at their kids' high school graduation.

"Cute," Maggie managed around the annoying lump in her throat. She wasn't sentimental, but it was hard to ignore the love and pride shining from Annie's eyes. "What are their names?"

Amanda took another look at the pictures, her expression shuttered. "Who's watching them while you're here?" she asked, almost accusingly.

Annie stared at her, the smile slowly dying. "My best friend is enjoying time with Chris and Daniel. Jared's mom drops by every day to make sure they're all right." She gathered the pictures and shoved them angrily into her bag. "I assure you, Jared and I are good parents. We wouldn't leave them with just anybody."

Amanda flushed. "I apologize. It's just... with the things I've seen... you need to be careful, that's all." She rubbed her left arm and turned for the door. "I think I'll see if Mrs. Stein needs a hand. See you inside." The screen rapped the doorframe as it banged behind her and then the door softly closed.

"That went well," Maggie muttered, her gaze moving from the house back to Annie. "I don't think she meant to upset you." And why she was defending SAC Rhinehold was anyone's guess. Maggie sensed the woman didn't like her. She had a feeling it had something to do with Adam, but her life was too screwed up to worry about it.

Annie pulled a face and picked up her cup again. "I shouldn't have taken offence like that. It's just... with Jared being gone all those years, I've learned not to put up with crap, you know?"

Oh, she knew. Maggie's backbone had cost her plenty.

"Well, we should go eat before the men get back and steal it all," she said, smiling to relieve the tension. She might need a rest from this mini-vacation before it was over.

7

Nick Kelley hung up the phone on a deep sigh and sat back, ignoring the old desk chair's groaning complaint. The open calendar on his computer was a glaring reminder of how slow business was. If they didn't pick up some cases soon, his and Jared's fledgling P.I. business would be over before it had a chance to begin.

He rubbed his face and rose to cross to the coffee station his wife had carefully set up for him. Sara was so damn proud of him. She'd even designed their logo—Case Closed. He hated the thought of letting her down. Truth was, he didn't know what he'd do if the company failed. He still had some life savings—he wasn't dumb enough to sink everything into this venture—but he really didn't want to go back to carpentry work. He wasn't getting any younger, and with two kids to put through college...

At least Jared had sounded relaxed on the phone. When

their old commanding officer, Frank Stein, called asking for a favor, both men agreed, ready to drop everything for the Chief. Then Sara reminded him he'd promised Jessica he could participate in the Boys and Girls spring break camping trip. Who'd have thought the ex-marine would become a club leader? He didn't mind, really. It gave him quality time with his stepdaughter, and Jared's son, Chris, was fun to be around. It would be good for Jake, as well.

As though the Shepherd read his thoughts, Jake looked up at him from his bed near the door and let his bushy tail thump the floor.

"Five days, just you, me, and a pack of pre-teens. What could go wrong?" Nick bent to give the big head a fond rub. "Good thing you're trained for disasters." Not that anything was going to happen. They were staying in a monitored campsite and there would be a different parent volunteer for each night of the trip. But Caleb had been fussy lately and Sara was caring for Annie and Jared's toddler, too. It bothered him to leave her alone, though Jared's mom promised to drop in and check on them regularly.

The glass door with their company logo—a magnifying glass embedded with Case Closed—swung open, revealing Tidal Falls' sheriff, Jack Garrett. "Nick, how's it going?"

Jake sat up and whined but stayed put until Nick gave the hand motion to greet their guest. He rose and padded across the light hardwood floor to nudge the sheriff's hand.

"It's quiet, but we expected that. It'll take a while for word to get around."

Jack nodded and rubbed the dog's silky brown ears. "How you doing, boy? Don't worry, won't take long and you'll have your hands full." He shut the door and wandered toward the coffee bar. "Got any coffee left? Had a call early this morning and didn't get my quota."

"Help yourself." Nick's pulse kicked up a beat, but he played it cool. No sense letting the man know how bad he wanted in on the investigation. He waited until Jack had his cup and settled onto the leather sofa before approaching the subject. "So, uh, what sort of call?" He couldn't believe he was actually hoping for a major crime—jeez.

Jack quirked a brow and blew on the steam rising from his mug. "Something you're not telling me?"

"No!" Nick raked a hand through his hair. "Believe me, I've learned my lesson about withholding valuable information from the police." He'd almost lost Sara to her psychotic ex-husband because of it. "I was just thinking, maybe, we could collaborate on the case. You know, like partners?" Most law enforcement officers didn't look kindly upon private investigators, but Jack was different. He cared more for his community's safety than protocol.

"Partners, huh?" Jack scratched a whiskered chin. He unzipped his windbreaker, revealing the shiny oval badge on his white button-down dress shirt, and crossed one jean-clad knee over the other. "Well, I *am* short-staffed at the moment.

Walters went and pulled a hamstring while running a marathon—the idiot—and Sid is visiting family in New Brunswick. Normally, I'd suffer through, but with spring break around the corner, I don't want trouble."

He set the cup down and leaned forward. "Between the two of us, the men we're looking for are dangerous. The sooner we get them behind bars, the better."

Nick swallowed hard and glanced at the framed photo of his wife and kids hanging behind the sheriff's head. He'd do whatever it took to protect them. It sounded as though the camping trip was going to have to be put on hold. Jess wouldn't like that, but he didn't see a way around it. Better she was disappointed in her dad than possibly in danger from an assailant.

"What did they do?" he asked, referring to the suspects they were looking for. He liked to have as much information up front as he could. In his experience, it was the unknowns that generally tripped a guy up. He rubbed his damaged leg absently and focused on the grainy photo Jack had unfolded from his pocket. Two men in orange jumpsuits stared back at him, their eyes dark with animosity.

"Escapees?" he asked, staggered by the implications.

Jack nodded, his expression grim. "From William Head Prison just over the border in Canada. Best we can figure, they swam across the inlet, holed up in a farmer's cabin—the man was found dead from a gunshot wound a week later— then stole a boat and gained entry into Washington along the west coast. Task force members found the vessel hidden in a cove under a tarp, leading us to believe they have outside resources.

"There's been no sign of them since then—until this morning. The department received a 911 call from the Tranmere residence. Jenny said she was woken by her dogs going crazy at the back door. She called us first—smart girl—then snuck downstairs with a can of pepper spray in hand."

Nick swore. "She should have barricaded herself in her room. Damn, Jenny. Is she...?"

Jack threw the wanted poster on the table and rose to pace the too-small room. "She's safe, no thanks to her recklessness. I've warned her before that it's not safe to stay on that farm by herself, but she won't hear of moving into town." He stopped near the window, the ambient light through the blinds sending dark stripes across his body. "The good news is that she did agree to a couple of bruiser dogs— Rottweiler crosses. They scared off whoever was out there. She caught a glimpse of two people running down her driveway, one bulky, the other tall and slim."

Nick stared at the photos on the table. A.J. Davis; six-five, broad as a football player, tribal tattoos starting on top of his bald head and sliding down the right side of his neck to disappear under the garish orange prison uniform. The second inmate; Dennis Floyd Allen, six-one, rail thin, ropey muscles, shifty eyes and pockmarked skin. Intimidating for anyone to come across, never mind a young woman. When he'd first arrived in Tidal Falls, Nick was attracted to the cute, friendly hairdresser, but his heart had already been given to Sara. He hated to think of Jenny facing those criminals alone.

"What were they in prison for?"

Jack frowned. "Police raided Allen's home and found a stash of drugs and weapons valued at over thirty million. Davis was caught leaving the scene with a kilo of Fentanyl and a replica semi-assault rifle. Both men were known to have connections with organized crime on the mainland."

"I want in on this," Nick stated. This was his home. Sara, Jessica, and baby Caleb deserved to live without fear, and he was going to make sure they were safe.

"I was hoping you'd say that," Jack said. He walked over, hand out. "Glad to have you on board. Want to be my deputy?" he teased.

Nick grinned and took the sheriff's hand in a firm shake. "Want to be a gumshoe?"

Not what he expected for a first case. Guess he was about to get his feet wet.

8

F rank held half a turkey sandwich, his mood melancholy as he gazed over the land his family had lived, loved, and worked for generations. There'd been many challenges over the years, from droughts to floods and everything in between. There was even a memorable occasion when the famed frontiersman Davy Crockett and his volunteer unit stopped at the ranch for a warm night's sleep and a hot meal during the winter of 1835 on their way to an ill-fated siege at the Alamo mission.

"You going to eat the rest of that?" Jared asked.

"Are you kidding me?" Adam grouched.

"What? I'm hungry." Jared, again.

"Why didn't you eat breakfast, then?"

"I wasn't hungry, *then*. I'm hungry now. Besides, by the time you filled your plate, there was nothing left for anyone else."

Frank turned away from the peaceful view and eyed his friends. "You two sure you're not a couple?" He tossed his lunch bag across the grass in their direction. "Have mine. I'm not eating anyway."

Jared started to reach for the bag, until Adam nudged him in the ribs. "Ow," he cried, rubbing the spot as though he'd been mortally wounded. "What did you do that for?"

"Because you're an idiot, that's why." Adam gave him a disgusted look. He took a drink from his tin coffee cup and lifted his chin toward the far range. "How much land do you have out here, Frank?"

"Hey, that's Chief to you, bozo," Jared said, diving into the lunch bag and coming up with a bright red apple.

"Almost a thousand acres with eight hundred head of cattle. It's a full-time job." *And it's in my blood.* Frank found it hard to reconcile the kid who'd run off to join the navy with the person he'd been when he came out of the teams. If he'd learned anything overseas, it was to value the things that mattered, like peace and serenity. His gaze settled on each of his SEAL brothers—his family. Without their loyalty and strength, he wouldn't be here.

"Shit, no wonder you look grumpy," Jared muttered around the fruit in his mouth. He held up his hand before Adam could elbow him again. "I'm kidding, jeez. Where did your sense of humor go, O'Connor? If that's what it takes to become a DEA agent, leave me out."

"Not a problem," Adam said complacently. "They only

allow people with high IQ's into the organization." He grinned as Jared sputtered. "Besides, you have a wife and kids to worry about. You wouldn't be happy traipsing all over the country."

"True that," Jared agreed. "What about you, Frank? Do you miss the thrill of the chase?"

Did he? Traipsing through rat-infested jungles, spitting dust in the desert, HALO jumping in the thick of night... Sure, he missed the adrenaline rush. But, the other side of that coin was facing their mortality. Kill or be killed; a phantom following every op, but they trained for it. Too bad it wasn't as easy to rid themselves of the nightmares. PTSD—painful, tortured suck-ass dreams—or Post Traumatic Stress Disorder, as his psychiatrist termed it. Frank called it the end of his career.

"Nah, this place keeps me going. That shit is for the young guys, ones with something to prove. I did my time."

"Hell, yeah. You saved our asses more often than I could count," Jared said. He held his arms out. "Want to bring it in for a hug, guys?"

Adam threw his empty sandwich wrapper at Jared's chest. "I can't believe you've made it this long with a straight nose."

Jared grabbed the bag, crumpled it and shoved the garbage in with the rest. "Jealous, pretty boy?"

"Not of you," Adam answered equably and turned to

Frank. "I can see the draw to ranch life. Wide open spaces, peace and quiet, the satisfaction derived from a hard day's work—it's tempting, man. This last investigation, and what happened to Maggie, it's made me reevaluate, you know?"

Every time Frank thought about what Magdalena had gone through, he wanted to bring that Mexican drug lord back to life so he could torture him to death. It didn't matter that she was trained to survive the kind of sadistic brutality Chenglei had inflicted, it changed a person. Frank just hoped his home would help to heal the wounds on her soul.

"I'm always looking for a good farmhand," he told Adam, rising to stretch his legs and walk off some of his pent-up anger. *As long as you forget about renewing your relationship with Maggie.* He liked Adam—had trusted the guy with his life—but he'd had his chance. Magdalena needed someone who could appreciate the amazing, resilient person she was now, not a guy who reminded her of who she'd been.

Frank planned to be that man.

***

Maggie poured thick, warmed, maple syrup over her hot cake before accepting a platter overflowing with bacon from Frank's mother. "Thank you, Mrs. Stein. You didn't need to go to so much bother."

"It's Emily, dear. We don't stand on formality here." The

older woman smiled and dunked her wedge of toast into a soft-boiled egg. "I enjoy cooking, it gives me pleasure. And besides, they say food is the way to a man's heart. It certainly works in this house."

"Well, I know Jared appreciates your home cooking." Annie added a strawberry compote to her stack of two hotcakes. "I tend to burn everything I cook." She laughed.

"Frank's father liked to share the story of my bread-making foibles when we first married. He swore he used the loaves to build our deck out back." Emily chuckled.

Amanda held up her slice of toast and gave it an appraising look. "I'd say that's not a problem anymore." She lathered raspberry jam over the top and took a bite, her eyes closing in pleasure. "Can I move in?"

Maggie bristled, even though the pretty agent was obviously—probably—teasing. "How would you run the field office from here?"

Amanda slowly set the toast on her plate and wiped her fingers on a napkin before meeting her gaze. "I was hypothesizing, Agent Holt. You must know what that's like. After all, you *imagined* yourself head of the department when you ignored a direct order and almost got yourself killed. Isn't that true?"

"That's not how it happened," Maggie growled, aware of the other women's startled expressions. She pushed away from the table and rose. "Thanks for breakfast, Emily, but I've lost my appetite. I think I'll go outside and blow off some steam." *Before I say something I'll regret.*

"Hold up, Agent. I'll join you." Amanda thanked Mrs. Stein, as well, and followed Maggie out the door and down the stairs into the yard.

"What is your problem?"

Maggie shot a sideways glare at the thorn in her side. "I don't have a problem. I just think you should concentrate on our investigations instead of the Stein ranch." *And Frank.* She'd already picked up on a weird vibe between Amanda and Adam. How many men did she need in her web?

"First, they aren't *ours,* you're on paid leave, remember?" Amanda lowered a pair of stylish aviator sunglasses over her eyes. "And second, I was simply being nice to our hostess. There was no ulterior motive, so I don't appreciate getting called out like that."

Maggie strode toward the brook, barely able to take in the natural beauty of their surroundings over the turmoil in her heart. *Had* she overreacted? Her therapist warned it would take time before she could properly reintegrate into society. Too much had happened, her brain and hair-trigger emotions had to work themselves out. Maybe she'd be better off out in the wilderness somewhere on her own—without a weapon or she was liable to shoot some poor hunter's head off. In short, she couldn't trust her own reactions. Lovely.

She owed her boss an apology. "I'm sorry, I don't know why I said that. I guess I'm not the best company right now."

Amanda nodded. "I understand. You've been through a traumatic experience, but that doesn't give you leeway to treat those around you like crap. You're still a DEA agent, Holt, act like one."

Maggie refrained from clicking her heels but couldn't resist the raised brow she leveled at the other woman. "We're off-duty, remember?" They stopped on the gently rolling bank and stared at the murky brown depths of the water. It reminded her of a slithering serpent in the garden of Eden, and she gave an involuntary shiver.

"In our line of work, there's no such thing," Amanda murmured just as her cell phone gave a strident ring. "Excuse me," she said, reaching into her pocket for the thing as she stepped away for some privacy.

Maggie noticed a small cabin nestled under an old oak tree like a sleeping cat. Its boards were gray with age but seemed to be in good repair. A big stack of split wood ran the length of one wall, and a couple of weathered Adirondack chairs sat out front facing the creek. This must be the place where Frank was staying while she occupied his room at the house. It suited him somehow. Alone, yet warm and welcoming. A sanctuary.

Until Amanda's voice interrupted the serenity. "That was head office. They received some disturbing reports from this area about possible narcotics dealers. They want my team to look into the matter." Amanda stared across the field to where cowhands moved purposely between the corrals and outbuildings. "It seems that even in the most peaceful locations, you have to watch out for snakes."

The brackish brook burbled its agreement.

9

It was late afternoon by the time Frank and his companions rode into the ranch grounds. Hereford cows and their calves scattered as the horses trotted across the pasture. "Branding season," he said by way of explanation. Some cattlemen had changed from the old technique to ear tags and tattoos but, given the value of his purebreds, Frank preferred sticking to tried and true methods of identification. Not that it had stopped thieves from raiding his herd.

Spencer raised a hand from his perch on the top rail of the corral. One of their horse wranglers stood in the center of the pen guiding a frisky filly on the end of a long rope in a wide circle.

"Nice looking horse," Adam said, riding alongside. "Thoroughbred?"

"Yep. See that gray?" Frank pointed toward the stallion

tossing his head and pacing the fence line two pens over. "He's the future of our breeding program. Horse racing is a lucrative business. Who knows, we might even raise the next Derby winner."

"So, you're diversifying?" Jared asked, from his other side. "Good plan. Spread and conquer, no pun intended."

"Yeah, something like that," Frank acknowledged, though it was more of a last stand situation. With rising ranch costs and lowering beef prices, he needed another source of revenue to protect the land.

Dismounting, he led Sadie over to Spencer, Adam and Jared following suit.

"How's the ride?" his foreman asked, spitting a wad of tobacco juice into the dirt.

Frank frowned. "I thought you were giving that shit up?" Spencer was in his late sixties. He needed to start taking better care of himself.

Spence wiped his mouth with a less-than-clean rag and stuffed it back into the breast pocket of his western shirt. "Don't you be tellin' your ma. I only have one or two chews a day. Man needs to have his dip."

"You aren't in the major leagues, buddy. Those guys are half your age and *they* shouldn't be doing it either." Ever since they'd attended that Rangers game years ago, Spencer had taken up mimicking the players by chewing tobacco. Go figure.

"Bah." Spence waved his hand in the air like he was

swatting a fly, then pushed up the brim of his cowboy hat. "You only live once." He nodded toward the greenhorns. "You'll be wanting a hot bath tonight or you'll find aches and pains in places they shouldn't be—if you get my drift." He winked and chuckled.

Jared rubbed his left butt cheek. "Already do. These saddles should come with air ride suspension."

"Hey, that's not a bad idea," Spencer said. "Write that down, Frank. Something to think on."

Frank shook his head good-naturedly. "Yeah, not happening." He rested his arms on the rail and watched the filly go through her paces. "She's looking good. Tomorrow, I'll try saddling her up."

"You boys are in for a treat. Frank, here, is a legend in these parts when it comes to breaking a horse. He has the touch."

"You a horse whisperer, Chief? A man of many talents." Jared slapped him on the back.

"What the hell is a 'horse whisperer'?" Adam asked, staying clear of the dust swirling out from under the filly's dancing hooves.

"You ever been out on a romantic date, young man?" Spencer squinted down at Adam.

"Of course," Adam answered with an uncomfortable snicker.

"Well then, you get the gist of it. A good trainer knows how to woo the horse. Show it he doesn't mean it no harm.

He has to pay attention to their body language, act on the queues. Treat the animal with respect, earn its trust, and it will submit." Spencer swept his hat off his balding head, slapped the brim against his thigh, then lowered it over his eyes.

"Am I the only one who needs a cigarette now?" Jared asked, ever the jokester.

"I just listen to my instincts. It's not that hard," Frank said.

"Speak for yourself," Jared muttered, staring at the feisty horse in the ring. "You wouldn't catch me within ten feet of those hooves."

"Finesse, Martin, something you're not exactly known for." Adam nudged Jared's shoulder. "Good thing Annie doesn't mind a bumbling neanderthal in the romance department."

Frank snorted and waited for the fireworks to go off.

Three.

Two.

"I have plenty of romantic moves and two kids to prove it. If that means I'm a neanderthal I'll take it, you baboon."

Blast off.

Adam hunched into his collar, his expression transforming into the facsimile of a primate's grimace. "Not cool, man. You know I'm sensitive about my short neck."

It was true; for a guy who was often mistaken for a movie star, Adam had little self-confidence. Frank stepped between their squabbling before it degenerated into a grudge match. "I don't know about you, but all this lovey-dovey talk is making me hungry. Ready to go up to the house, ladies?"

Jared wrapped an arm around Adam's neck and squeezed. "Hell, yeah. This guy needs a banana." He laughed and danced out of reach before Adam could land a punch.

"You're such a dick," Adam said, grinning at his friend.

"See you up there?" Frank asked Spencer.

"Yeah, sure. I'll just keep an eye on these two until they're done." He nodded toward the pen and the now still horse, its ears twitching and honey-brown coat quivering with a fine sheen of sweat.

"Make sure he gives her a good cool down," Frank directed.

"Will do, boss."

"You and Nick have the new business up and running yet?" Adam asked Jared as they led their horses into the barn.

"Just about. We're going to do a grand opening and promotional push when Annie and I get back to town." Jared tied his horse to a metal ring in the aisle and started in on the buckles and straps holding the saddle in place. "It would be great if you and Frank could be there. We couldn't have done it without you."

Frank handed each man a curry comb and ran his over Sadie's dusty back. "I'll be there, Magnum."

Adam chuckled. "Next he's going to want a Lamborghini."

"Well, since you offered," Jared said, returning from setting the saddle on sawhorses set up for that purpose. "My birthday's in May, buddy."

"In your dreams," Adam murmured, staring at his cell phone with pinched brows.

"Everything okay?" Frank asked, removing his jacket. Sadie rattled her bit and gave him the eye over her shoulder as though to say, "*hurry up, it's dinner time.*" He patted her rump. "I know girl, I know."

"It's Amanda," Adam was saying, tap-tapping a message on his cell. "Looks as though the party is over—we have a case."

Frank's stomach plunged. They'd be going then and taking Magdalena with them. "When do you leave?"

Jared met his gaze, sympathy in the depths of his blue eyes. "Maybe Maggie should stay here for a while. You know, detox."

Adam looked up and frowned. "She's not a druggie, for crying-out-loud. Mags is staying with me—we're partners." He shoved the phone in his pocket and looked at Frank. "I have a feeling we just found your vandals. Amanda says there's a drug ring in the area with ties to the Renegade movement and the Mexican mafia. This could blow up in our faces if we aren't careful. Never a dull day, huh?"

Frank swore. He'd heard of the Renegade Resolvers.

They were a fundamentalist movement gaining strength with right wing groups seeking to overthrow the government. Add in a lethal cocktail of drugs shipped over the border from Mexico and they had themselves the makings for a civil war. All in his backyard.

Hooyah.

10

J essica Sheridan sat cross-legged on her bed frowning at the clothes falling haphazardly from her school backpack. Guess she might as well plan on a *boring* spring break, since the camping trip Nick *promised* to take her on was canceled.

Oh, it wasn't official yet, but Jess knew. She'd eavesdropped on a phone conversation her mom had with Chris' mom and overheard the bad news. It wasn't fair. They'd planned this trip for months and now all the other kids in the Boys and Girls Club would hate her.

She flopped backwards, her hair a poufy cloud around her head and stared at the ceiling, dreaming of hazy blue skies and Anthony Henderson in swim shorts. She'd never felt like this for a boy before; kind of warm and shivery at the same time. It sucked he was a year older and had started at a different middle school this year while she was stuck in dumb old Jubilee. It was the main reason she'd convinced Chris to join Boys and Girls with her—to get closer to Anthony.

Her cell phone beeped an incoming text message. She rolled onto her side and stared at the neon green case like it was a snake. She didn't have many friends; her father had left a lasting impression, and now, thanks to Nick, she wouldn't have any.

But instead of some kid's rude comments, it was Chris.

U hear the news?

Jessica's finger hovered over the keys. Did she want to have this conversation right now? She sighed. It wasn't Chris' fault her life was about to implode—again.

Is it too late to homeschool?

Lol. It won't be that bad. There's always next year.

Says you.

Chris didn't get it. He was eleven, things were easy then. Grade seven was different. Harder. Girls who talked to her before suddenly ignored her, or worse, made fun of her boobs. She looked down at the offending bumps and tears trickled into her hair. This was supposed to be the trip that would make the unpopular girl the one everybody wanted to hang out with.

Instead...

Have you talked to your mom?

What good would that do? She was bound to side with Nick.

She's busy with the babies. That much was true. Her little brother, Caleb, was crawling now and into everything. On top of that, Mom and Nick were babysitting Chris and his baby brother, Daniel, while their parents visited a friend in Texas. Maybe *she* could move to Texas. That *might* be far enough away to avoid the rest of her teenage years.

Hey, Jess?

Yeah? Who else did he think he was texting? Jeez.

We could go camping—just us.

She sat up in a rush. Could they? The last time she and Chris had tried anything alone, they'd been kidnapped by a Russian mobster. Her heart fluttered like a thousand butterflies trapped in her chest. It was a crazy idea. On the other hand, if they pulled it off, maybe it would be enough to redeem themselves with Anthony and the rest of the group. Prove they were independent, cool kids who could get away with flaunting parental control.

The cotton-candy pink walls and ruffled curtains keeping the inky darkness at bay mocked her hesitancy. Her mom had gone through a lot with her father, and because of that, she tended to treat Jess like a child instead of an almost teenager. She barely let her go anywhere without adult supervision—jeez.

She typed, *Let's do it*, just as a quick knock had her scrambling to hide her phone under the pillow. Her mom opened the door with a tentative smile.

"Hey, kiddo, doing okay?"

Jess shrugged and lowered her eyes, scared her mom would know she was up to something. "I guess."

Mom joined her on the bed, right beside the hidden cell phone. "Nick feels bad, honey, but he didn't have a choice. He had to cancel the camping trip."

The guilt she'd been feeling disappeared in a rush of hurt. "I'm going to be a laughingstock," she wailed.

"Oh, I don't think it's that bad, is it?" Her mom wrapped a comforting arm around Jess's back. "We'll do something fun later, maybe invite the club over for a picnic—how does that sound?"

Like she'd be the only one attending. "Yeah, sure. Hot dogs in the backyard, they'll love the idea."

Mom squeezed her shoulder before letting go. "Sarcasm doesn't become you, young lady. We're doing the best we can. Everything can't always go the way you want them to, it's how you react that counts."

Things never went her way, but she planned on changing that, starting with her secret camping excursion with Chris. Anthony had to take notice of her after that.

"I guess. I'm tired, Mom. I think I'm going to go to sleep now." It was hard to keep quiet. She normally shared everything with her mom, but lately, with the baby and all, Jess kind of felt like a third wheel. Then again, she'd been moody ever since she started getting her period—whoever said the menstrual cycle is something to celebrate, was nuts—so, that didn't help.

"Okay, honey, but think over what I said. See you in the morning. Sweet dreams." Mom rose and walked to the door. "Maybe you and Chris can ride down to Grace's for ice cream tomorrow."

Jess's pulse jumped. That's when they could leave. No one would miss them for at least an hour or two—long enough to get to the campsite if they rode hard. She refused to contemplate how much trouble they'd be in when Nick caught up to them. She'd worry about that later.

"We'll probably stay down there for a while, if that's okay? Grace pays us to help out when they're busy."

"Oh, she does, does she?" Mom smiled. "I guess that means I can stop giving you an allowance then, huh?"

"Mom, that's not funny."

"Who's joking?" she said, then chuckled and closed the door, leaving Jessica to her guilt-ridden thoughts.

11

M aggie spent the morning dreading what her Zoom appointment with the company psychologist had revealed. Her word was final on clearing Maggie for work, and, so far, they hadn't seen eye-to-eye on much of anything. The woman was a mental surgeon, digging and scraping all the detritus hiding in the dark corners of Maggie's mind. Stuff she'd worked hard to bury; stuff that had the ability to flay her alive if she let it escape.

Eager for a distraction, she strode down to the horse pens in search of the gray she'd seen earlier. Men nodded politely as they hurried by, intent on their daily duties. She envied them. At least they had something to focus on, she was like the tumbleweeds they'd seen driving up from Austin, floating along at the will of the wind.

Cows lowed in the distance, calling to calves separated

out for the branding iron. Maggie turned away, unable to watch the violent procedure. In a large corral, near a barn that stretched across the land like a sleek limousine, a group of men, feet resting on the bottom rail, arms folded across the top bar, observed a sleek chestnut-colored horse glide around the ring, its hooves barely touching the ground. She was fascinated by the skillful display shown by the cowboy standing in the center of the pen, a long rope the only thing guiding the spirited animal.

A shrill scream and stampeding hooves raised the hair on Maggie's arms. She knew that call, had heard it in her childhood dreams—it was the stallion.

Leaving the men behind, she followed her instincts and hurried down the endless length of the brick-red barn to a fenced enclosure. Instead of the sandy soil in the other pen, this one undulated with lush green grass. At the other end of the field, the king of his domain, the gray stallion tossed his elegant head and sniffed the air, deciding if she was friend or foe.

"*Orenda*," she murmured, for the horse truly seemed to have a magic power over her. Slowly, careful not to make any sudden moves, Maggie bent to pluck some of the long green grass growing next to a fence post.

"Hungry, big guy? Come on, I won't hurt you." She reached through the rails with her offering and waited to see if the ghost horse would accept.

He pawed the ground in response to her voice, then

reared, his hooves scraping the air, before galloping out of view.

Discouraged, Maggie let the grass slip from her fingers and stepped away from the fence. How silly to think this beautiful creature was the same animal who had protected a frightened girl in her dreams. The psychologist would have a field day if she found out—not that Maggie planned on telling her. She had a feeling the woman already thought she was *loco*, there was no need to prove her right.

It was nice back here. The barn provided a buffer from the busy front yard, letting the harmony of nature seep into her veins. Birds chirped as they flitted here and there, foraging for their dinner while the breeze sighed content-edly, rubbing arms with long grass fronds in a delicate dance across the field. Maggie closed her eyes and let the sun warm her face, relieving the tension in her neck and shoulders. Frank should promote his land as a therapeutic retreat, he'd make a mint.

"What brought that on?"

As though thinking his name summoned him to her, Frank stood in the shadow of the tall barn doors, watching her.

"Hmm?" she murmured, bemused by his appearance. He cut a commanding figure in his cowboy garb of worn denim jeans that lovingly hugged muscular thighs, a shear-ling jacket in a deep ochre, and a dusty hat pulled low over his eyes. Her pulse fluttered to life.

"The smile," he said, easing closer as though she were one of his untamed mustangs. "You don't do it often enough."

It faded now, scared off by guilt and memories. The breeze kicked up, her hair creating a screen between them and she was slow to sweep it back. "I haven't had much reason to smile, lately."

He nodded and stared off across the pasture. "Healing takes time. Some never recover from ordeals like you've been through. Don't be so hard on yourself, you did the best you could."

Did she? Maggie lived those endless days and nights in her nightmares. She kept thinking, if she'd only made different choices early on, Olga and the others would still be alive. It haunted her, the wondering—the self-doubt.

Not ready to talk about any of it, maybe ever, she returned to the fence and rested her arms on the top rail like she'd seen the horse wranglers do. "I tried to befriend your stallion, but he wasn't having anything to do with me."

"He's a beaut, isn't he?" Frank joined her, though he leaned his back to the rails and continued to study her expression.

"What?" she said, turning to face him. "Do I have dirt on my nose?"

His lips quirked. "Maybe I just like to look at you." He tapped her nose with a calloused finger. "But yes, you have a smudge."

Gasping, she tried to vigorously rub the dirt away, then slowed when she caught him openly grinning. "I suppose you think that's funny?"

"A little," he agreed, unrepentant. "It got you to loosen up though, didn't it?"

Self-conscious, she brushed a few runaway strands of hair behind her ear. "You're not what I expected," she admitted.

He removed his hat to run a hand through his own tobacco-brown locks, then looked at her with soothing pewter gray eyes. Whoever said gray was a cold color?

"That's funny, because you're everything I expected—and more." With those enigmatic words he turned to the pasture, lifted two fingers to his lips and gave a piercing whistle that rattled the wildlife as much as Maggie.

"What was that for?" she asked as the birds took flight. Her heart was pounding so hard she grasped her chest to keep it in place. Why did he say things like that? Was he trying some weird psychobabble stuff on her to *supposedly* get rid of her PTSD? She wouldn't put it past Rhinehold to use any resource available—she'd done it before.

A moment later, her foreboding disappeared as the stallion appeared on the horizon, limned against the white gold of the late afternoon sun. "*Orenda*," she whispered.

"You named him?" Frank asked, glancing at her in wonder.

She shrugged. "It fits." The horse pranced down the hill,

his mane and tail flowing out in an ebony banner heralding his arrival. "It means *Magic Power* in Iroquois."

Frank smiled. "Let's hope you're right. I have a lot riding on this guy." He reached into his pocket and removed a shiny red apple. "Here. Hold it in the palm of your hand—like this." He took her hand and placed the fruit, warmed from his body, into her grasp. "Good. Now hold it out and take some slow, easy breaths. In through the mouth, out through that cute, smudged nose of yours." When she turned to give him a few choice words, he shook his head. "Na, ah. He'll sense it if you're tense and take off before you can say boo. Save your retorts for later, Agent Holt. Right now, you have a horse to tame."

Maggie smirked, surprised by how much fun she was having with the tall cowboy. No wonder his teammates had followed him into the pits of hell, *he* was the magician.

Orenda closed the gap between them, head tossing as he neared. The apple proved too much of a temptation though, and, delicate as a sparrow's wing, he plucked it out of her hand leaving only the moist warmth of his breath on her wrist to prove he'd been there.

Frank spoke in a low, hypnotic voice, congratulating the big horse on his good manners, his beauty, his virility. The dark eyes with their impossibly long lashes watched them as though he understood everything and, of course, agreed. Chunks of apple broke apart under the bite of strong, yellow teeth and fell to the ground. Unconcerned with the humans now that he knew there was no danger, *Orenda* dropped his head and cleaned up every scrap, his forelock falling over his forehead.

Now that he was closer, Maggie could see he was more of a dappled gray, with dark speckles fanning out over his rump and back legs. His mane and tail, by contrast, were midnight black and thick and coarse. Without thinking, she reached out to pat his neck and startled him into jumping sideways with a snort.

Frank grabbed her wrist and yanked it through the rails just as *Orenda* snapped at her fingers. Trembling at the suddenness of the attack, Maggie dove straight back to the hell of Chenglei's Mexican prison.

12

F rank used his hat to scare off the stallion, cursing himself for not taking more care. The animal had never been properly trained. The previous owners hadn't considered it a necessity for his stud services, and, with the trip to Mexico and everything else going on with the ranch, Frank had let it slide. Because of that, his guest, *Magdalena*, had almost been injured.

As the horse kicked his heels and galloped away, Maggie folded to the ground at his feet, her arm twisted awkwardly where he held her wrist. Long, black silken hair flowed over her shoulder and breast, hiding her face from his view. He let go, grimacing at the red marks he'd left on her delicate skin.

Dropping to a knee so he could better see her expression, Frank frowned. She was pale, fragile looking. He didn't think the horse had a chance to hurt her, but with the way he'd yanked on her arm, maybe *he* had. "Are you injured?" he asked, roughly.

She lifted her head at the sound of his voice, but her eyes looked through him and suddenly, he realized why.

"Maggie, look at me." He carefully tucked her hair behind the shell of her ear. "Come back to me, sweetheart. I've got you." He rubbed her shoulder and was relieved to see her eyes lose that vacant, faraway expression. "That's it, take it easy. You're safe." And she would remain that way if he had any say.

Tears formed and she blinked them away. "I... I must have tripped," she said, her voice gaining strength as she raised her armor, blocking him out.

Much as he wanted to confront her with the truth and force her to talk to him, Frank understood the need to hide the flashbacks away—pretend they didn't exist.

He rose and held out his hand. "It's the stallion's fault, he startled you."

She accepted the offer and stood with less than her normal grace. "Thanks, I'm not usually so jumpy." She avoided eye contact while carefully brushing dust from her slacks. "I guess I was expecting more manners after we gave him an apple and all." Her wobbly smile begged him not to make a big deal out of her breakdown.

"It was my mistake, actually. I should have warned you about Desert Dancer. He's new to the ranch and still learning his boundaries. He's a showoff for the ladies—kind of reminds me of O'Connor."

Maggie lifted a brow. "Does Adam know how you feel?"

He grinned, pleased the sparkle had returned to her beautiful topaz eyes. "He'd be the first to agree. Back on the team we called him our secret weapon because he always managed to get intel for our ops when no one else could."

"Well, can't say I'm surprised. He made use of those... talents in the DEA, as well." She started walking and Frank fell in alongside. "It's kind of strange being here, with you. Adam used to talk about the great Frank Stein all the time. You're a legend, you know." She slipped him an intimate, sideways smile that set lightning bugs buzzing in his chest.

"Pretty sure that's a myth. Each member of a team is critical to its success as a whole."

"Wow, are you sure you aren't in politics?" She laughed.

Frank's lips quirked. "That bad, huh?" He opened the side door on the barn and stood aside so she could enter. Her arm brushed his as she passed, and the effect on his body was instantaneous. Her easy laughter flowed over him like a midsummer night's breeze; warm, seductive, and addictive.

"Listen, Maggie, I was thinking, while you're here, maybe we could—"

"There you are. We thought we might need to send out a search party," Adam called from near the front doors. "Nice way to get out of work, Chief."

Jared exited a horse stall, straw stuck to his clothes.

"That would be your specialty, O'Connor. Where did you disappear to when it came time to pack those hay bales?"

"I was taking a phone call, buddy. Duty calls." Adam glanced outside as though he was looking for someone, then turned and strode back into the dim barn. "Amanda is on the way. She needs to talk to all of us, and it seemed serious." He shrugged. "She's the boss."

***

Maggie had a feeling she knew what Amanda wanted—the use of Frank's ranch. If they remained as his guests, they would be less likely to raise suspicion while running their investigation into the drug ring. Anger flared. Frank loved this ranch. It was wrong to bring the kind of malicious criminals Amanda knew operated within these organizations to his family home. She wouldn't allow it.

She grasped Frank's arm and a thrill of awareness rippled down her spine. "You don't have to do anything you don't want to."

Frank looked down at her with a surprisingly intense expression. "If you're involved, I want to."

She gasped, her heart beating like a runaway train. What was he saying? Was Frank Stein interested in the damaged, needy person she'd become? How could that be possible when she didn't even like herself? "You don't mean that. I'm a wreck. Didn't you hear? I'm not even fit for duty, or so my esteemed psychologist claims. You'd be better off kicking the lot of us off your property and electrifying the gate." It was probably the only way he would keep the DEA from taking over.

"Are you offering advice or a warning, Agent Holt?"

At Amanda's tart voice, Maggie closed her eyes and sighed before turning to face her annoyed boss. "Whatever it takes, I guess. You and I both know it's dangerous for the Steins to have us set up shop here."

Amanda parked her hands on her hips, Adam and Jared bookending her like a couple of muscled thugs. "I told you, there *is* no us. You are relieved of duty until further notice. The only reason you're here now is thanks to the generosity of our host." She smiled at Frank and Maggie was selfishly pleased he barely acknowledged it.

"Magdalena is welcome on the ranch any time," he said, and glanced at his watch as though she was an irritating delay to his day. Amanda stiffened at the implied censure. "I understand you had something important you wanted to say?"

Jared changed sides, strolling over to casually take up a spot on the wall near Maggie. "Use your poker face," he murmured out the side of his mouth. "You're letting her know she's getting to you."

Maggie gave him a grateful nod and straightened out her expression to neutral boredom. Funny to think she was receiving advice from a man she'd interrogated a lifetime ago.

"Just get on with it, Amanda. It's been a long day and I,

for one, could use a beer." Adam scowled at Jared and Frank but remained next to SAC Rhinehold.

If this were the OK Corral, it would be obvious who the lawmen were.

Amanda glanced around, then moved closer as though she was about to divulge a state secret. "Is there somewhere more private to talk? What I have to say is highly sensitive information."

Frank frowned. "This is as *private* as you're likely to get around here, Ms. Rhinehold. My men are outside and it's a big barn..."

Amanda's eyes flashed. She didn't like not getting her own way, but she'd better get used to it. Maggie planned on being her fly in the ointment for this op.

"We've been tracking the movement of a fundamentalist group going by the moniker of Renegade Resolvers. They began as a white power, antigovernment organization back in the 2010s and have since spread throughout the US. They gained notoriety after the Black Lives Matter movement when they started calling for a race war. Between our presidential issues and the violence erupting everywhere, the Renegade Resolvers believe it is a call to action. They want to start a civil war, overthrow the government, and bring about a complete societal collapse. These people believe it is the only way to rid our nation of the *so-called* filth."

"Why Renegade?" Jared asked, a length of straw clasped between his teeth.

"It was a code word in the second world war," Amanda replied. "The problem is further complicated by another faction within the organization who are fundamentalists and don't believe in racism. Some have ties to Antifa—anti-racist groups who monitor and track neo-Nazis. We can't just go in and do a mass clean up, even if it were possible, or we'd face a barrage of legal claims."

She crossed her arms and paced the floor, sending dust motes dancing in the shaft of light streaming through the open doors at the far end of the barn. "The radical wings of this faction are little more than homegrown terrorists. We stopped a plot to bomb a hospital last month, Lord knows what they have planned next."

"I understand the issue," Frank said, his voice a low rumble, "but what does it have to do with the ranch?"

Amanda stopped, met Maggie's warning glare, and lifted her chin. "The DEA would like to set up an investigation in the area. We believe the Renegade Resolvers are using drugs to support the cause and convince their followers to take extreme measures when called upon. We know there is a shipment of methamphetamine, heroin, and cocaine slated to arrive in San Antonio later this month. We need to stop that delivery before it gets to distribution. And we believe you can help us do that."

Frank gazed at Amanda for a long moment before raking his hand through his hair. "Well, hell. I left the teams to get away from this crap. Seems it followed me home."

Maggie's heart plunged. She knew what he was going to say and tried to forestall it. "It's late. You all must be starving, I know I am." She gave a nervous laugh. "Let's go up to the house and give this a rest. We don't need to decide anything tonight, do we?"

Adam regarded her with worried eyes. "You should go back to Vegas. Your damn cat is destroying my furniture, take him home."

Her cat. It had been so long since she'd held him. But she wasn't going anywhere until this situation was rectified. There was no reason they couldn't set up shop in town. It would be easier to monitor comings and goings of strangers anyway.

"I'll hang around for a bit. Besides, your furniture needs renewing." She smiled to let him know she appreciated his concern.

"I'm not sure how long Annie and I can stick around, but I'm happy to kick some ass until then," Jared said.

"So, it's decided then." Frank tipped his hat back and leveled them all with a grim look. "You can stay here and do what you have to do, but only if we're included in the operation. And that means Magdalena, too."

Maggie stared at Frank in shock. He'd gone to bat for her. Instead of locking her up in a padded room and throwing away the key until they caught the perps, he was ensuring she got her second chance. Her silly pulse leapt, partly from fear, but mostly because someone—Frank—had shown faith in her.

"Well, this should be fun," she said brightly to a glowering Rhinehold. Hopefully she wouldn't get anyone else killed.

13

N ick pulled up in front of Grace's Café and shut off his engine. He had an appointment to meet with the sheriff at seven. They planned to have breakfast, then do a search of the area surrounding the Tranmere farm for the missing convicts. Unless they'd managed to get their hands on a vehicle, the men couldn't get far. Check points were set up on the only road leading into and exiting Tidal Falls. The region was mountainous and thick with towering evergreens—unless they were mountaineers, he had a feeling they were holed up somewhere waiting for an easy out.

Sara and the babies had still been asleep when he'd left, one heart-stoppingly beautiful, the other two sweet and innocent. He hated leaving them, but the high-tech security system Jared had installed in their homes gave him some comfort.

It was a brisk spring morning and his breath left him in puffy white clouds as he hurried up the steps and entered the restaurant to the welcome aroma of fresh-brewed coffee and savory bacon cooking on the grill. A few other early risers glanced toward the door as it opened, and Nick raised his hand to familiar faces. The sheriff wasn't there yet, so he grabbed a booth alongside one of the table-to-ceiling windows and turned over his cup.

"What are you doing out and about at the butt-crack of dawn?" Sue cackled and poured his coffee from a steaming carafe.

Nick grinned at the feisty server. "You know I can't resist Grace's grits for long. How you doing, Sue?"

"Never better," she replied. "When are you bringing that baby of yours down here?"

"Soon. Sara can't wait to show him off. Maybe after Jared and Annie get back, we can all come down for dinner." He stirred a couple spoons of sugar into his coffee.

"That's right, Grace said something about Chris and little Daniel staying with you while they took a trip to Texas. Guess you have your hands full, huh? You need help, just give ol' Sue a call. I love those kidlets."

"Will do." Nick raised a hand to catch the sheriff's attention as he pulled up outside. "It's been too long since you and Grace stopped by. Sara would love to see you."

Susan turned over another cup and filled it, then moved

aside so Jack could take a seat. "Morning, Sheriff. Having your usual?"

Jack removed his hat, scrubbed a hand through flattened hair, and smiled. "You know me too well." He nodded toward Nick. "You order yet?"

"I'll have whatever he's having, Sue, thanks." Nick waited until she moved away to serve other customers before getting down to business. "Any word yet?"

Jack undid his leather jacket, took an appreciative sip of his coffee, then leaned back and eyed him over the rim of the cup. "Nah, but I figure they have to come out of hiding sooner or later. We'll get them."

"I hope you're right, Sara's worried." Nick checked his phone, but there were no messages. "Her father is in prison. This brings back bad memories for both of us." He never wanted to relive the fear of seeing her in the hands of a madman again.

"Has she heard from him? You don't think these two—"

"No, and no, of course not. Why? Is there something you're not telling me?" Nick glanced around the restaurant, before leaning forward. "You have to admit it's suspicious. Why would two escaped criminals go out of their way to come here, the very same town where a well-known lawyer for the Sinaloa Cartel was arrested? Coincidence, or...?"

Jack sighed. "I was afraid of that. Any ideas?"

Sheridan's Phoenix File came to mind. "Maybe. I have to check on a few things." Nick sat back as Sue arrived with their breakfasts. "I'll get back to you on that." He needed to reach out to his DEA friend and see if there were any updates on the investigation.

"Here you go, gentlemen. Anything else I can get you for now?" Sue set the plates down and reached into her apron pocket for a package of gum. "Not quite the same as smokes, but it's helping me to quit."

"Grace finally talked you into it, did she?" Jack grinned and picked up his fork. "Got any hot sauce back there?"

Sue nodded. "Sure thing, and just so you know, it was *my* decision to quit. Grace gets enough credit around here." She stomped away, her blonde beehive hairstyle leaning precariously to the right.

"Now you did it," Nick said, shaking pepper over his hash browns and eggs. "Don't you know you're never supposed to irritate the people who feed you?"

Jack chuckled. "Women. I don't think I'll ever figure them out. I told Lauren I liked her new shoes the other day—even though she has like a hundred pairs—and she got all ticked and informed me they were at *least* three months old, as if I could tell."

Nick shook his head. "Sometimes, it's better not to say anything at all, rather than make an idiot of yourself—just saying."

Jack gave him an ironic look. "Gee, thanks, ol' wise one. Any other inspirational tidbits you'd like to share?"

Sue plunked a bottle of hot sauce on the table and

refilled their coffee cups—up to the brim for Jack—then bestowed a sweet smile on Nick. "Grace said she'll be out to see you as soon as this rush settles down. She'd like to take the kids on the weekend to give you and Sara a break. And before you say no, I'll be there to help. The older ones can watch over the younger babies. We'll be fine." She patted his shoulder, gave Jack a sidelong *watch-it-buster* look, then moved on to the next table.

"So," Jack said as he shook the hot sauce onto his eggs, "you going to let them go?"

Nick's eyes watered and his nostrils burned from the acrid aroma. "You're going to burn a hole in your guts with that shit." He coughed on the fumes and sat back to give them a moment to evaporate. "I don't know. Four kids are a handful for anyone. Grace and Sue are kind to offer, but until we get a handle on these convicts, I'll feel better if the family stays together."

"I'm the same way. I don't much like Tina managing the Craft Shack while Annie's away, but she's old enough to make her own decisions. All I can do is make sure this town is safe for my daughter and every other person who counts on the sheriff's department—even you." Jack pointed his bread knife at him before spreading some of Grace's home-made cherry jam on his toast.

"You should run for mayor next, you've got the jargon down pat." Nick added jam to his own toast, took a bite and closed his eyes as the fruit exploded on his taste buds. "I wonder if she'd adopt me," he murmured.

"I already have," Grace said, strolling up to the booth, her face flushed. "Whew, that kitchen is hot. Slide over, this old lady needs to get off her feet for a bit."

Nick hurried to comply, his shoulder bumping the cool glass as he made room for Jared's mother. "Delicious, as always," he complimented her cooking prowess.

"What brings two of Tidal Falls' most handsome men out so early in the morning?" she asked, cutting to the chase.

Jack exchanged a cautionary glance with him before smiling at Grace. "Most handsome, huh? I'm already a regular, you don't need to butter me up," he teased.

Sue sidled up to the table, the ever-present coffee pot in hand. "Did you get anything to eat?" she asked Grace.

"Quit mothering me," Grace answered good-naturedly. "I had some oatmeal before the rush started. Did *you* eat anything?"

Sue frowned. "I'm not the diabetic. Do you want some coffee, or don't you?" She lifted the glass carafe in front of her.

"What bee got into your bonnet?" Grace muttered, accepting the cup Nick passed over.

Sue filled her cup and topped up the other two, then picked up the empty plates. "I have no idea what you're talking about. Stay put for a while, we can handle things for a bit."

"Yes, ma'am." Grace took a fortifying sip of her coffee. "Lord, I needed that." She raised her brow at Nick. "So, are you going to try and hornswoggle me, too?"

Nick's glance slid to Jack and away. "No deception, Grace. Jack and I are looking into a possible collaboration between Case Closed and the police force. It would be a beneficial partnership for the both of us."

"Well, sure, I can see that," she said, setting down her cup. "Sue mention that we want to take the children for the weekend?"

Relieved she'd let the matter go, Nick smiled. "Yes, she did. Are you sure it wouldn't be too much for you? Caleb is crawling now." His smile slid into the grin of a proud father.

"It's not that long since Chris was little, I'm sure we can manage for one night. Now, you plan something special to show that beautiful wife of yours how much you love her." She looked at Jack. "How's Laurel these days? Is she enjoying her new job?"

"She's loving it. It was nice of Rebecca to recommend her at the school when an opening came up."

"She's a sweet girl. When are you two going to give Tina a brother or sister to spoil?"

Jack choked on his coffee.

Nick chuckled. "Nice one, Grace. I don't see him at a loss for words very often."

"Just putting the thought in his head, if it isn't there already." She winked, then glanced around the busy restaurant. "Well, duty calls." She heaved herself up with a sigh. "Whatever it is you're up to, take care of yourselves, you hear?" She waited until they acknowledged her command before shuffling back to the kitchen.

"How did she know?" Jack asked, shaking his head.

"Psychic," Nick answered. He threw a couple of twenties on the table. "Ready to catch us a convict?"

"Hell, yeah," Jack agreed.

14

A dam trailed the others up to the farmhouse, his thoughts in turmoil. Maggie wasn't ready to go back to work, why couldn't anyone see that? She was going to get herself killed. If he thought it would do any good, he'd throw her under lock and key until this investigation was over. It was too much. She was close to breaking and he wasn't sure what he'd do if he lost her again—maybe for good this time.

His gaze bore a hole in Amanda's slim back as she strode up the hill with Frank on one side and Mags on the other. Her hair had slipped from its bun to tumble down her spine in a riot of sable-colored curls. It made her seem softer somehow—more approachable. Until you came up against her professional side. There wasn't another Special Agent in Charge like her. She ran their field office as one of the best in the country, and it was the very reason he resented her; she didn't let personal feelings enter the equation. Everything Amanda Rhinehold did was geared toward making the United States of America safe for the citizens who called it home. Commendable, really. Unless you were on the opposing side of one of her decisions—like now.

Jared glanced back, then slowed to wait for him. "What are you moping about?"

Adam stiffened. "I'm *not* moping, as you so politely put it. Maybe I was enjoying a bit of peace and quiet, you ever think of that?"

"Huh, I never took you for a liar. All those years in the DEA soften your backbone?" Jared tipped his hat back and gave him a cocky smirk.

"You're lucky I'm tired, Martin, or I'd show you how soft I am. Why don't you go bug your buddy up there and leave me alone." Adam usually appreciated Jared's quick wit, but that fiasco in the barn had him on edge.

Jared sobered. "Look, if you have concerns, the Chief deserves to know about them. Is there a credible danger to his family?"

Adam gave him an irritable look. "Hell, why ask me? Amanda runs the show."

"But she's not one of us. Come on, O'Connor, you owe the team your loyalty." Jared tossed the straw he'd been chewing off to the side.

Yes, he was well aware he wouldn't be here if his teammates hadn't risked their lives to rescue him from an ambush.

It was a debt he could never repay, and it weighed on him every single damn day. That, and the guilt he carried like a mantle for withholding the fact he'd already been on a mission for the DEA when he'd joined the Team. A member of FAST, or Foreign-Deployed Advisory and Support teams, his job was to search out a suspected narcotics division working within the military. And it almost got his team killed.

He'd been fighting the bad guys, one way or another, for most of his adult life. It might be time to step aside, let someone else bear the burden for a while. But first, he had to protect his friends from Amanda's single-minded deter-mination.

"Amanda, can I have a minute?" he called, aware of Jared's frustrated sigh beside him. Until he hashed things out with his boss, there wasn't much he could say to reassure the others.

The three in the lead stopped and turned, each with differing expressions. Amanda radiated impatience, Maggie curiosity, and Frank suspicion—not that he could blame him.

"I hope you know what you're doing, man," Jared muttered, moving to join Maggie and Frank as they continued up to the house.

"Me too," Adam said under his breath. He waited until the others disappeared inside, then gestured for Amanda to lead the way down to the riverbank.

"I know what you're going to say, and the answer is, I had

no choice." Frogs croaked in the background and iridescent blue dragonflies skimmed the murky water's surface as Amanda faced him with crossed arms.

"Just the fact you're already on the defensive tells me that's not true." Adam wanted to remain annoyed, but she looked stressed enough for both of them. "Why here, Amanda? It would make more sense to be in town. How can we keep an eye on anything in the back of beyond?"

"It's hardly the back of beyond," she said. "Look around, what do you see?"

Adam knew what he'd see, acres and acres of green pastures, wildflowers, cows and cowboys. It was about as far removed from his Las Vegas home as it could be, and yet he felt an affinity for the land, a bone-deep connection that surprised him.

So, instead he concentrated his attention on Amanda, taking in her vibrant beauty against the vivid backdrop of a setting sun. Her features were almost sharp, instead of classical, with almond-shaped green eyes, upturned nose, and full, sensual lips that featured in way too many of his dreams. Ever since their passionate kiss on the hill when Maggie was missing, he hadn't been able to get her out of his head—or treat her with the distance and respect she deserved as his superior officer.

"I can't see anything but you," he admitted softly, drawing a surprised gasp.

"You can't just say things like that," she cried, fingers

cupping her throat as though to hold all the words she wanted to say inside.

"Why?" he asked, suddenly tired of pretending there was nothing between them. He grasped her hand, tugging her off-balance and into his arms. "It's true. We have a connection, Amanda. One I want to explore. Are you going to deny the attraction I see in those beautiful green eyes?"

She lowered her lashes, blocking her expression from his view, but he could feel the rapid-fire beat of her heart, the trembling in her limbs, the moistness of her barely parted lips. She wanted him just as desperately, he was sure of it.

"Amanda," he murmured, lifting her chin. "Look at me and tell me I'm imagining this—us—and I'll never mention it again." He waited, half hoping she would do just that. End this craziness before it ruined both of their careers and broke their hearts. He'd been through an office affair before, with Mags, and look where it put them now—strained partners who couldn't get past the distance separating them.

"I can't," she whispered, opening her eyes to gaze up at him. "But that doesn't make it right. I've worked hard, damn hard, to get to this position. I can't allow a temporary affair with a fellow officer destroy my reputation. Not even for you."

Not even for you.

She cared. He'd hoped he wasn't alone in this relationship and here was the proof. Even as she attempted to turn him away, she'd opened a tiny gap in her armor. Satisfaction warmed his veins and put a smile on his lips. "It's too late, boss, I'm hooked."

He bent and kissed the disbelief from her lips.

***

The moment their lips meshed, Adam knew he'd made a mistake. He thought he could control the allure of a short-term affair with Amanda to help him get over Maggie, but it wasn't going to be that easy. The moist warmth of her mouth sent his heart catapulting in his chest. His blood sizzled with the urge to take her down to the thick green grass and bury himself in her core, but he forced himself to take it slow, to savor the soft skin of her cheek beneath his fingers, the swell of a full breast against the palm of his hand. The erotic sound of her voice sighing his name.

"Adam..." She opened eyes filled with desire, deep green pools he could happily drown in. "We can't do this."

"Why not?" he murmured, nibbling on her jaw. "We're free agents. Why can't we have a little fun?"

Her eyes narrowed and the soft, pliant body turned into a post. "That's what this is to you, *fun*?" She stepped back, allowing in a draft of cold air to cool his ardor—or maybe that was her frosty expression.

He raised his hands out at his sides and shook his head. "Of course not. You're taking my words out of context.

Kissing you *is* fun, Amanda. And sexy, and irresistible, and addictive—should I go on?"

"Please, do. I haven't seen a charmer in action before, it's... enlightening." She sighed and straightened her blouse, mussed from his touch. "Can we get back to business now?"

It was his turn to sigh. "Running away won't solve our issues, but sure, boss, I can wait."

Her eyes telegraphed her relief and he suddenly realized the indomitable SAC Rhinehold was shy. She faced the day-to-day challenge of their job with such confidence and passion, it surprised him to think of her as uncertain in any aspect of her life. But, then again, he didn't remember her ever having a relationship in the time they'd worked together.

"Amanda..."

She quit fidgeting with her clothes and raised her chin. "Yes, Agent O'Connor?"

Seriously? After having their tongues in each other's mouths, she was going to pull rank? Incredible.

"Never mind, it isn't important." He kicked a loose stone and watched it plonk into the water, causing a ripple effect that reminded him of why he'd asked her here. "I don't think it's fair of you to use my friendship with Frank to force him into letting us take over his ranch for an op that could bring danger to his family."

"And," he swiftly added when she opened her mouth to reply, "I want Maggie far away from any of this. You've seen her, she isn't ready to return to duty. I can't believe you're even considering it."

Amanda—*SAC Rhinehold*—frowned and glanced toward the ranch before stiffening her shoulders. "I'm not used to having my orders questioned, Agent, but in this case, I'll grant you some leeway. Your friend, Mr. Stein, strikes me as an intelligent man. One who knows what to expect and yet elects to help because he recognizes having an organization such as these people out on the streets is dangerous to everyone.

"Believe me, if I thought there was another alternative, I would use it. But this ranch is central to where we think the exchange will occur. This is our best chance, and we're taking it. End of story."

She nodded toward Maggie, who'd come out on the porch and was watching them with a hand raised to her brow. "Agent Holt is stronger than you realize, Adam. Maybe you need to have some faith in your partner." She stared at him for a moment longer, then turned and strode up the path to the house.

Adam watched the two women exchange a few words, then Mags waved and followed Amanda inside, leaving him alone with his thoughts.

He turned back to the stream with its deep undercurrents and wondered how long before it dragged him under.

15

I t was full-on dark by the time Brian decided he'd better go to town and babysit the idiots he had to work with. If it was up to him, he'd leave Lennox and Jenkins to drink themselves stupid, but with their big mouths they could ruin the entire operation and send the three of them back to the pen. Brian would kill himself before that happened.

"Where are you going, son?" His mother shuffled into the kitchen just as he was sliding on his black corduroy jacket.

"Out for a drive. I need some air," he hedged.

"Well, don't be gone long. You know your father." She tightened the belt on her faded pink robe and filled the kettle before setting it on the stove. "He's happy you're home."

Sure, he is. The car keys bit into his palm. "Okay, Mom. Don't wait up."

He made his escape while she bent to light the stove, the crisp air clearing the acrimony from his chest. Returning home wasn't easy, but those years behind bars had taught him a valuable lesson—family meant everything. Even hardened criminals turned sappy on visiting day. Not that he'd know what that was like, his parents hadn't shown up once in the five years he'd stayed in that hellhole. But the past was the past. He planned on showing his worth this time around. Just as soon as he paid this debt to Rivero.

The headlights picked out the fence posts like ghostly sentinels down the long length of the gravel driveway and a sickle moon dangled in the velvet sky draped in diamond dust. Another thing he'd forgotten; how big everything appeared in the Texas countryside. It was tempting to keep on driving, just disappear into the great unknown and let the chips fall where they may, but his family would pay the price for his cowardice and he couldn't do it.

The ride into Huntersville went by fast and too soon Brian was pulling up in front of the town's only watering hole, the Pickled Pepper. Incandescent lightbulbs only lit up part of the sign leaning drunkenly on the rooftop, leaving strangers to guess what the last two p's were. That, along with the heavy wooden doors, made the place seem less than welcoming. Still, the bar used to do a thriving business, especially on a Friday night. Going by the vehicles lining the street and the music shaking the walls, tonight was no exception. Again, Brian wished he could just keep driving.

Sighing, he shut off his car and headed for the bar.

The raucous noise hit him square in the chest, followed by the rank odors of hot, sweaty bodies and spilled beer. It was a sensory overload after the controlled chaos of prison life. If he hadn't spotted Jenkins' ugly chops at a billiard table in the back of the room, he would have turned around and left. Instead, he pushed his way through the crowd, keeping his head down to avoid getting noticed. At one time, he used to be well-liked around here, before he'd succumbed to the temptation of drugs. He wasn't anxious to explain himself to his neighbors when he hadn't even made amends with his own family yet.

"Well, lookee there. Our old pal, *Brian*, arrived just in time to pick up our tab," Lennox brushed past with a sardonic smirk, two bottles of beer in each hand.

Damn Lennox.

"Leave him alone, man. What's your problem?" Jenkins chalked his cue and leaned over the pool table, eyeing Brian as he lined up his shot.

Great, Lennox was a belligerent drunk. *This should be fun.* Aloud, he said, "It's cool. Let's see if he can put his money where his mouth is." He nodded at Lennox as the other man set the beer down with a clunk. "Best out of five buys?"

Lennox obviously thought that was hilarious. He chortled so hard, he coughed his fool head off. Rubbing the spittle from his lips, he pointed to the table next to the one Jenkins was at. "Beat it," he snarled at the two men playing.

"Jeez, Lennox, are you for real?" Brian shook his head and removed his jacket. He couldn't afford to waste money on that asshole's drinks. "Hope you're ready to cough up some dough along with your lungs."

"You're a riot, Finch. No wonder Rivero kept you all to himself." Lennox's gray eye glinted maliciously while the brown one stared at him with a flat gaze that creeped him out.

"Shut up, you idiot." Brian glanced around, but no one seemed to be paying them any mind. "If he knew you were throwing his name around, he'd cut your tongue out and feed it to you on a skewer." The jerk was going to get them arrested. Rivero didn't get to where he was without making enemies—on one side of the law or the other.

"Rack 'em up, *B.J.*, I can't wait to wipe your ass." Lennox grabbed a cue and tested its weight like he was a frigging pro.

Brian winced. He hated that nickname. "Aw, I didn't know you cared." Trying to look more confident than he felt, he set up the balls and prepared to take his first shot. "Get ready to weep, I call solids."

Bam. The cue ball broke true and scattered balls across the felt. Yellow dropped, and a moment later, red rolled into the side pocket. Brian straightened and looked across the table to get Lennox's reaction. The other man had a bottle of beer up to his lips and took a long swig before setting the brew down and swiping at his mouth.

"Lucky shot. Careful or I might think you're cheatin', and you know what happens then."

Yeah. He'd get the living shit beat out of him. He suddenly lost his taste for winning and sluffed the next shot. "Your turn."

They were starting to attract a crowd, either drawn by curiosity, or because they could sense the animosity Lennox wore like a thorny cloak and wanted to be in on the fight. That was the thing with drunks in a bar, they were always ready for a little action to spice up their night.

Brian pulled his cap lower over his eyes and kept a scowl on his lips, daring anyone to come closer. So much for his plan to get these two out without causing a scene. All he needed now was for the law to walk in.

"Brian Finch, is that you?"

Or the nosy old foreman from the Bella Vista spread.

Aware of Lennox and Jenkins' narrow-eyed gazes, Brian turned to greet his neighbor. "Spencer. It's been a while." He looked the same, lean and lanky with a grizzled gray beard and weathered skin.

"It surely has. Your pa mentioned you were getting—" Spencer glanced around and cleared his gravelly throat, "home soon."

Surprised, and grateful, for the other man's sensitivity, Brian gave him a real smile. "I can imagine how *that* conversation went." His dad would be happiest if he hadn't been born. "How's Mrs. Stein doing?" He remembered she'd lost her husband due to a freak accident a few years before he went into the clink.

"She's good, great actually. Now that Frank is managing the ranch fulltime, she and I..." He stopped, his cheeks reddening.

The old codger. Everyone knew Spencer Tate carried a torch for Emily Stein. Looks like he was finally doing something about it. Melancholy settled as Brian contemplated his lost chances.

"You playing, or what?" Lennox growled from behind him.

"You're kind of a rude dick, ain't ya?" A belligerent drunk flicked one of the balls on the table, sending it bouncing off the others.

"Hey, watch it," Lennox snarled, slapping the cue onto the table and jostling more balls. "Who do you think you are?"

"Calm down, man. It don't matter." Jenkins left his game to step into the fray. He reached out to clamp a warning hand on Lennox's arm and got a punch to the nose for his efforts. "What the...?" he howled as blood poured over his lips and chin. "You stupid sonofabitch, that hurt." He tried to staunch the flow by cupping a palm over the injury, but deep red drops landed on the green felt, staining the fabric.

The drunk near Brian didn't like that and picked up a

ball to pelt it at Lennox. The ball glanced off his shoulder, eliciting a low roar that built like a freight train.

Lennox shoved Jenkins out of his way and scrambled around the end of the table, murder in his mismatched eyes.

"You better get out while you can," Brian warned Spencer as the crowd surged. He was tempted to turn tail, as well, but couldn't until he got those lamebrains out of here before the cops arrived.

"Jenkins," he yelled over the brawl. When he caught the other man's attention, he pointed toward the back door. "Go," he mouthed.

Jenkins hesitated, his already black eyes on Lennox. Then he shrugged and turned his back on both of them, disappearing into the mob.

One down, one to go.

Brian took a fortifying breath and dove into the tussle.

F rank reined Sadie in and dismounted, leading her down to the pond for a drink. They'd been out for hours, combing for strays and checking fences. A cowboy's life could be lonely, but he reveled in the peaceful solitude. Or he did when his mind wasn't so torn.

He crouched and soaked his bandana to splash the refreshing water on the back of his neck. It was a beautiful blue-sky day. A pair of eagles soared high above him on the wind currents and for a moment he wished he could drift up there with them, but the ranch's issues would still be here, so he settled back on his heels, poured a tin cup of steaming coffee and contemplated his recent decisions.

Last year, he'd tied a big chunk of their assets into the new horse breeding program that may, or may not, get off the ground, and now with the downturn in the cattle industry, it was a financial burden the ranch couldn't sustain for long.

And then he'd gone and given in to temptation by inviting Maggie Holt to his home. She'd looked so lost when they found her in Mexico—as though a vital part of her soul had vanished. He couldn't stand to see her that way. Back in Vegas she had radiated energy, a livewire that jolted his heart with her vivacity. He wanted to help her heal, to see that spark again. But not at the cost of his family's safety. Ask any of his SEAL brothers and they would agree, impulsive decisions were as rare for him as snow in July. Yet here he was, allowing a government investigative team to basically use his land as bait—not exactly a brilliant move, even for Magdalena.

"What do you think, Sadie girl? Did I make a mistake?"

She stopped chewing the tender shoots of grass growing along the bank and gave him a solemn look from chocolate brown eyes.

"Is that a yes?" he asked, then shook his head. "I guess if I have to ask my horse for advice, I have my answer."

Sadie blinked long, dark lashes and went back to grazing, leaving Frank to drink his coffee. "You're right, I'm over-thinking it. We've been through worse than this and survived —I'm sure we'll do just fine." His gaze was drawn to the top of the knoll where an old oak tree stood watch over generations of Steins laid to rest beneath her graceful boughs, flush with lime-green spring leaves.

After tying his horse to a nearby shrub, Frank climbed the short hill and removed his hat before opening the black wrought iron gate to the family cemetery. His great-great grandparents, grandparents, aunts, uncles and cousins, all resided within the fenced area, but it was his father's tombstone that drew him today.

> Friend, husband, father
> Protector
> Frank Stein Sr.
> Born 1955- Died 2004
> Gone but never forgotten

There was a vase filled with fresh flowers and he wondered if his mother had been up recently. He made sure the graveyard was well cared for but didn't spend much time here himself. It brought on too many feelings, ones he fought to contain. Guilt. Loss. Remorse. None of which would bring his dad back. Didn't stop him from wishing things were different though.

He rested his hand on the smooth marble and closed his eyes. *I'm trying, Pops. I'm trying.* Warmth infused his chest, expanding his lungs until he thought he would rise above the trees like one of the helium balloons they'd had as children. Cam used to let his go on purpose, saying he was sending it to kids who didn't get balloons for their birthdays. That was Cam, the giver. He'd always placed others needs ahead of his own and it ended up costing him time and time again until he just... disappeared. If Frank had known the secret his brother tried so hard to hide back then, maybe he could have helped. Instead, he'd been so busy following in Frank Sr.'s footsteps, he'd missed Cameron's distress. And it was an ache Frank carried. Every. Single. Day.

"I thought I saw someone out here. Where's your horse?" Spencer's gravelly voice drew him out of his bittersweet memories and back to the issues he faced today.

One look at his foreman's face brought on a string of curses. "What the hell happened to you?" He gave his father's gravestone one last pat, then centered his hat on his head and strode through the graveyard to gaze up at Spencer sitting somewhat awkwardly on his horse. "Someone finally kick your ass for you?" The other man was sporting a split lip and a swollen cheekbone and looked as though he'd thrown down with a gorilla.

Spencer cackled and ended up coughing and holding his side as he groaned. "Something like that. I ain't as young as I used to be." He slid out of his saddle with a soft *oomph*. "Your ma was worried about you. Sent me out to have a look. I don't think she's feeling none too sympathetic at the moment."

"So, I'm guessing that means this is self-induced?" Frank shook his head. After all the enforced fighting he'd done in his career he couldn't understand why anyone would invite trouble.

"Don't you start in on me now," Spencer growled. "All I did was go into town for a quiet beer at the Pickled Pepper.

How was I to know I'd get jumped by some young whipper-snapper?"

Frank could have told him that there was no such thing as a *quiet* beer in a bar on a Friday night, but he let it pass. The old cuss had been through enough and it sounded as though Momma wasn't done giving him the gears over it. "Mom doesn't have much patience for drunks. Guess it's a good thing you don't make a habit of going to the bar—*do you?*" He hadn't noticed Spencer drinking much, but if he was...

Spence rolled his eyes and gathered up the reins. "If you're done acting like the boss of me—which you are, but not when it comes to my private life—I'm heading home to rest. Tell your ma she can apologize to me there." He grunted and groaned but managed to drag his sorry ass onto the saddle. From his lofty perch he looked down at Frank. "I respect your mother too much to upset her for no good reason, you should know that by now." He wheeled around and started down the hill.

Well, shit. Guess it didn't matter how old he was, he could still get taken down a peg or two. "Ice them ribs," he called to the man who'd practically raised him.

Spence pulled his horse up short. "Oh, yeah," he hollered. "That Finch boy, Brian? He's out of the clink and hanging with a couple of rough-looking dudes. Thought you should know."

Frank waved in reply and watched as Spencer galloped

away. That might be worth a follow-up; their farm butted Bella Vista's on her southern border, not too far from the shot-up signposts. The Finch clan had been in the area damn near as long as his own family, he'd even temporarily dated one of them a while back, before Maggie. He remembered the scrawny kid who'd gone to church services with his ma back when Frank still believed in such things—war sucked the Lord's teachings right out of a guy.

Time to have a sit-rep with his new teammates.

17

N ick pulled up in front of Jenny Tranmere's two-story gingerbread farmhouse with its wrap-around porch and glanced over at Jack. "Do I get to play good cop? That frown makes you an obvious choice for the other part."

Jack straightened, his leather coat creaking in the confined space. "I guess it was hoping for too much to come across Davis and Allen thumbing a ride on the way out here."

Nick shut off his engine. "Hope is a good thing, Sheriff. We just can't count on it to solve the case. You ready?"

Jack sighed and opened his door. "I'm the good cop."

Yeah, he was. That's why anything that went wrong in Tidal Falls bothered him so much. He'd taken a pledge to protect the town and did a damn fine job of it, too—though Nick didn't plan on telling him that. The cream-colored

Stetson he liked to wear barely fit his swelled head now. "Whatever you say. Just be nice to Jenny, she's a sweet lady."

Jack raised a brow but refrained from commenting. They climbed the wide plank steps up to the porch. Two high-back rocking chairs with thick flowered cushions sat to the right, under a broad window covered in lace curtains. It was a woman's house and Nick knew Sara would love it. His dream was to buy them a farm like this, one day. To raise their kids and grandkids with room to run. A place to grow old together.

But first, he had to make a success of Case Closed. He was proud of his wife's achievements as an artist, but Nick couldn't picture himself as a house dad. He'd considered using his time in the Marines to train military dogs, but after the injuries he'd suffered when that IED blew, he didn't think he could manage the long hours on his feet. Besides, chasing bad guys was what he and Jared did best.

Jack knocked on the door and the hounds of hell answered him from the other side. The wood reverberated under the force of the angry chorus. He stepped back, hand on his service revolver. "Some doorbell," he muttered.

Nick agreed. Not many would brave those snarls to enter without an invitation. He actually thought it was brilliant. Those animals had to be well-trained. They hadn't made a sound until Jack knocked, spurring them into duty.

"No wonder those guys took a hike," he murmured.

A moment later, the door slid open a couple of inches

and Jenny peeked over the chain lock, while two black noses sniffed the air from below. "Sheriff?" she asked, her gaze fearful. "Did you catch them?"

"Not yet," Jack replied, removing his hat. "We, Nick Kelley and I, were hoping to have a word with you—see if you remembered anything else about the encounter."

Nick moved so she could see him. "We won't take up too much of your time, Jenny."

Her eyes brightened and she closed the door, unhooked the chain, and ushered them in. "Don't worry about Bonnie and Clyde, they're harmless."

Jack stopped so suddenly Nick almost plowed into his back. Two King Rottweilers sat side-by-side, their beady eyes watchful as Jenny strode into a room off the hallway. "Umm, Jenny?"

Nick gauged the animals' calm demeanor and held out his hand so they could catch his scent. "Hello, you big beauties. I bet you take the job of watching your pack seriously, don't you?"

"Pack? Are you suggesting there's more of these brutes?" Jack paled.

Nick's lips quirked. There wasn't much that shook the sheriff's stoic attitude, but apparently intimidating dogs fit the bill. "I was talking about Jenny. How come you never told me you were afraid of dogs? You seem fine around Jake."

Bonnie and Clyde must have decided they were harmless; they rose as one and glided down the hall, disappearing from view.

Jack let out a gusty sigh and wiped his brow with a handkerchief he pulled from his pocket. "Jake doesn't look at me like I'm dinner. Let's go, get this over with." He marched after Jenny. Nick chuckled and followed, impressed with the oak floors and the vaulted ceiling in the family room they entered.

Jenny wore an oversized varsity sweatshirt over leggings, her blond hair in a messy ponytail—a sure sign the normally well-put-together stylist was shook up. She stood to the side of a large bay window, waiting. "It's been a while, Nick. How are Sara and the baby?"

Nick sat on a brocade sofa that was stiff as a board while Jack opted for a post next to a fireplace large enough to roast an elephant. "They're fine. Great even. And you, Jenny? I haven't had a chance to come in for a haircut in a while." It was only a little awkward talking to an old girlfriend about his new wife and child—just a little. He ran a finger under his collar and got down to business. "Listen, we appreciate you taking the time to see us. Jack told me about the scare you had, I'm so sorry." He glanced at Jack, who nodded for him to continue. "Can you run it by us again? Maybe there's a detail you missed that could help us locate those two before they get too far."

Jenny crossed her arms and moved to a chair, avoiding

walking directly in front of the window. Nick frowned. No one should be afraid to live in their own home.

"It was cloudy. It's always dark in the country, but that night... something felt off. Even the dogs wouldn't settle. Finally, I took them to bed with me and fell into a restless sleep. And then..." She paused, trembling fingers with long pink nails going to her throat.

"What happened next, Jenny?" Jack held a notepad and pen in hand, but his gaze was sympathetic as it rested on her pale face.

"A noise downstairs woke us. At first, I thought it was just the furnace coming on—it's been rattling lately—but it sounded like it was coming from the back deck, and the dogs were whining in front of the door." Her baby blue eyes had grown huge as the memories flooded back. Nick wanted to offer comfort, but Jack's glower held him in his chair.

"Was that unusual? The dogs whining like that?" he asked, leaning forward.

"What?" she asked, blinking. "Oh, yes. Bonnie and Clyde are normally very laid back. I've even had a bear in my yard, and they stayed calm. I guess they knew we were safe in the house, or something. Anyway, some glass broke—I found out later, it was from the windowpane in the back door—and they went nuts. I threw on a robe, grabbed the only weapon I could find, a flashlight, and opened the door. They took off, barking and snarling. And I followed, my heart wedged so hard in my throat I could barely breathe."

She looked at Jack. "I should have called for help. I know that. It just happened so fast and yet slow, too—like when you open your eyes under water, and everything is calm and quiet until you breach the surface and chaos erupts. One of the dogs cried out, and I froze on the stairs. But then I heard yelling and cursing and the dogs snarling, and I knew they'd scared off whoever it was, so I hurried after them and saw the men."

She wrung her hands and stared at the floor. "One was big, real big. He glanced back and fired a gun at Clyde, but missed, thank God. The other man was shorter and thinner —faster, too. He was way ahead of the first guy until he yelled for him to slow the hell down. I still hear his voice in my dreams—deep and gravelly. They were wearing some kind of orange jumpsuits like the type you see at airfields, or something.

"As soon as I knew for sure they were gone, I whistled for Clyde and went into the kitchen where I found Bonnie licking a wound on her side and the glass broken out of the back door. They almost got into my house, Sheriff, and they hurt my dog."

Nick rose and moved around the reclaimed wood coffee table to crouch at Jenny's side and take her hands. "You did just fine, Jen. You're incredibly brave, you know that, right?" He squeezed her fingers until she met his gaze. "You couldn't know what was happening or that those men carried guns. If you'd stayed in your room, they may have gained entry and it could have been much worse, okay?" He ignored Jack's warning growl and focused on her face. "I need you to think back. Did either of those men see you, Jenny? Did they make eye contact with you?"

Her eyes clung to his, a ship in a storm-tossed sea. "I... I don't think so, but it's hard to say for sure. I *was* looking out the window. I was scared for Clyde, and angry that someone had tried to break into my home. The fright came later, when I called 911 and the reality that I was basically a woman alone in a dangerous situation hit me.

"I hadn't turned on any lights—I heard once that it was better to keep the element of surprise—but I was carrying my flashlight, and I did have it on." Her gaze swung wildly from Nick to Jack, and back again. "Do you think they know who I am? Are they going to... to come back and kill me?"

Nick shook his head, even as his stomach dropped. "No, but to be safe I think you and the dogs should come into town and stay with Sara and me for a few days. Sara would love the company." He hoped. Jack raised his brow. Nick shrugged. He wasn't sorry he'd made the offer, but he should have run it by his wife first.

He rose. "I'm going to step outside and make a call while you get ready. You may as well come back with us now."

"But... my car. How will I get home? And what about the dogs?" Jenny looked stricken.

Jack stepped into the fray. "Nick's place is only a couple of blocks from downtown and your hair salon. They have a big fenced backyard for their German Shepherd and the kids. Are your dogs good with other dogs and children?"

Jenny smiled, some of the tension easing from her shoulders. "Oh, yes. Before they moved, my brother's family lived here at the farm. The house belonged to our parents and we inherited it when they..." She sobered. "Well, anyway, Bonnie and Clyde grew up around kids and adore them." She turned to Nick, her eyes warm. "I remember Jake, he's a sweetheart. I'm sure they'll get along just fine. That is, if you still want me?"

Talk about leading questions. Nick knew she didn't mean it that way. Jenny didn't have a devious nature. But with their history and Sara's post-pregnancy hormones, he may have bitten off more than he could chew. Only one way to find out.

"I'll be right back. With me and Jack working together, it'll only be a matter of time before those men are captured and life can get back to normal. We'll get someone out to fix that glass for you later today. How's your dog? Did you get it into the vet?"

"I took her first thing this morning, she only needed a couple of stitches. The vet found some glass fragments in the wound and figured she slipped on the floor. Are you going into law, Nick Kelley?"

Both of Jack's brows went up this time, whether it was her flirtatious tone or the thought of Nick joining the police force, he wasn't sure. Nick shot him a killing look and Jack smirked, the bastard. "No way. We'd probably end up shooting each other if I did. This is temporary. I've actually just opened a private investigation office with a military buddy of mine—Case Closed."

"Oh, I think I saw your office. On the corner of Fifth and Main?" She gathered a sweater laying on the back of a chair and moved toward the hall.

"Yeah, that's it. We have our grand opening next week. Maybe you can come?" *And tell all your clients.*

"Of course. It's a good idea, Nick. I'm sure you'll do great." She stopped, a slim hand curling around the door jamb. "Thank you. I didn't know how I was going to stay here without going crazy with worry." And then, she was gone.

Nick could feel Jack's gaze burrowing a hole between his shoulder blades. He turned and glared. "What?"

Jack smirked. "You sure like to flirt with danger."

Nick gripped his nape to ward off the headache that was threatening. "Someone had to make the offer," he muttered.

Jack nodded. "You're right. I'm just glad it was you." He chuckled.

Nick flipped him the bird and headed outside to call his wife.

18

Maggie sat at the back of the room, a part of, and yet separated from, the conversation going on around Frank's huge mahogany desk. He'd called this meeting after a long day out in the fields and looked tired, his craggy face strained. She didn't like the feeling that they were the reason for his stress. He'd done so much for her—them—already, it wasn't fair to keep taking advantage of his generosity.

Jared flopped into one of the burgundy leather accent chairs, a snifter of whiskey in hand. "I say we quit waiting for trouble to arrive and take matters into our own hands."

Adam glanced around until his gaze landed on Maggie before turning to Jared. "You know we need proof, buddy, or they'll walk. We need an ironclad case in order to take the group down and put them behind bars—hopefully, for a long time."

"What makes you think they're staying in the region? Is there intel you're not sharing?" Frank crossed his arms and stared Amanda down.

She cleared her throat and lifted her chin. "I'm not at liberty to discuss the details, Master Chief. You're not active duty anymore. We will try to keep out of your way and ensure there are no casualties while we are here. My team and I are more than capable of handling this operation, but... thank you. I appreciate your input."

Jared set down his glass and clapped, the sound discordant in the tense atmosphere that had descended on the room. "Great speech, ma'am, but if I recall rightly, you wouldn't have gotten very far without the Chief when you went to Mexico to rescue your agent not so long ago."

Maggie winced at the reminder of how her screwup had endangered so many and almost cost her life.

"That's enough," Frank said, his gray eyes soft on Maggie's face. "Fact of the matter is, if you want to play in my sandbox, I'm going to need you to make room for all of us. No offense, SAC Rhinehold, but my land, my rules."

Amanda looked as though she'd sucked a lemon, but she nodded and held out her hand for Frank to shake. "Deal, as long as you work under my command. All of you." She leveled them with a stern glance, stopping on Maggie. "And you, no more vigilante justice stuff."

"Amanda, for Pete's sake..." Adam scowled and strode over to perch on Maggie's chair. He put an arm around her shoulders and kissed her temple. "Ignore her, caffeine shortage."

Frank's unyielding expression turned even more rigid. "If we're done goofing off, can we get down to business? I still have a ranch to run."

Maggie stiffened and sat forward, dislodging Adam's arm. She appreciated his support, especially after everything they'd been through. But they were going to have to talk about their non-relationship and she wasn't looking forward to hurting him. They were unstoppable as partners, and best friends, but that's where it had to end. They were different people from the young hotshots who thought they could save the world.

Jared swirled the whiskey in his glass, holding the amber liquid up to the lamplight. "Does this group... what did you call them?"

"The Renegade Resolvers," Amanda supplied.

"The Renegade Resolvers. Do they have international ties? Where do they get their financing? What is their goal? How many followers do they have and what makes them so loyal?" Jared's eyes flashed with the same unholy glow as the alcohol and Maggie realized he was enjoying himself. Even more, he was in the zone—that place agents go when they're on the trail of suspected criminals—like dogs catching a scent.

Amanda wavered as though she was having an argument with herself over how much to divulge, before taking a seat and crossing her legs at the ankle. "Between the unrest over our government, job losses, and the death of Black Americans in custody, the extremist movement has been growing. There is evidence that this group is in Canada, Mexico, and many other countries spread across Europe."

She looked at Jared. "They are non-centralized, with a mixture of ideologies that align with neo-Nazis and anarchists. They believe it's their right to possess assault weapons, and dislike police and government with equal fervor. There are tens of thousands of them, and they're growing every day." Her gaze landed on each person in the room, adding weight to her words. "Many have military training, making it that much more difficult to arrest and charge them to the full extent of the law. That's not to say there haven't been convictions. Last May we performed an investigation into a bodybuilder in the Austin area. We found he was distributing steroids in central Texas and further up north in Lancaster. He used his social media platforms to advocate against the men and women patrolling Black Lives Matter protest rallies. At the time of his arrest, we confiscated multiple firearms, steroids, and call-to-action flyers he handed out at his gyms.

"The core strength of this organization is their ability to turn people into a version of suicide bombers. They work alone, or in pairs, and create chaos across our country, as well as our neighbors to the north. You may have heard of the Nova Scotia shooting rampage? Occurrences such as these create unrest and a need for change—a better world, at least in their eyes."

Adam had grown more and more tense as she went on, now he stood and faced her, fists clenched. "And what in Sam's hell do you think the five of us can do to stop them?" Maggie reached forward and placed a hand on his back to calm him down, but he shrugged her off. "Shouldn't we be coordinating with the other alphabet gangs? I don't like this. I don't like it, at all."

Maggie had heard enough. She knew where this was heading, she'd been there before. "You plan on cutting the head off the dragon, don't you?" Everyone, including Adam, turned at her quiet voice. Aware of Frank's intense gaze, she instead focused on her boss. "How big is the shipment?"

Amanda didn't mince words, an appreciative light in her eyes. "We're expecting at least twenty kilograms of meth-amphetamine, an undetermined amount of cocaine, and a load of firearms to be brought across the border sometime between next weekend and the following week, just in time for a protest slated for downtown Minneapolis. As I said, the group likes to operate with smaller resources, so we need to be on our guard for this. Whoever it is, they won't be easy to identify."

"Where are the drugs coming from?" Maggie demanded. A viper lay coiled in her stomach ready to sting. Adam must have sensed what was coming, he returned to his perch and clasped her cold fingers while she fought the darkening edges of her vision. "Who, dammit? Tell me."

"We believe it's the Texas-Mexican mafia with ties to the Sinaloa cartel. I'm sorry, Maggie. If it's more than you can handle—"

Maggie rose, holding on to her equilibrium by a thread. "I can handle myself, just fine. I already told you I'm ready for duty. Let's not get into that again." But, if she didn't get out of here now, she was going to make a fool of herself.

She forced a wobbly smile. "I'm bushed, not used to all this fresh Texas air, I suppose. If you'll excuse me, I'll see you all in the morning."

"I'll escort you to your room," Frank said, and there was something in his gaze that told her she'd better accept.

Leaving the heavy silence behind, she walked out of the room with the tall cowboy at her side. "I'm fine, you know. Your house isn't that big, I can probably find my way."

"Want a beer?" he asked abruptly.

She startled, surprised by the non sequitur. "Uh, sure?"

He grinned down at her and butterflies kicked the viper aside. "What's the matter, too young to drink?"

"Ha, ha," she said, feeling decidedly girlish. "A lady doesn't reveal her age. You'll just have to trust me, I guess."

"I should be the one telling you that. They mean well, you know, your friends. Unless you've been a POW it's impossible to understand. Give them a break and they'll come around."

She was getting dizzy with the emotional roller coaster this night had turned out to be. "What do you know about prisoners of war, Mr. Stein?" She *so* didn't want to have this conversation right now.

He stopped and gave her a disappointed look. "You don't need to build walls between us, Magdalena. I value your privacy. I just wanted you to know you're not alone. If you ever want to talk, or not, that's fine, too. And to answer your previous question, I do."

Maggie tilted her head, confused and just a little embarrassed. "You do... what?"

The heart-stopping grin made another appearance. "Trust you, of course. Now, let's get us that beer."

Bemused by an attraction she hadn't expected, Maggie trailed Frank into the kitchen, her worn-out state forgotten.

19

Frank sat at the kitchen table nursing a beer and enjoying the novelty of watching a woman eat like she was hungry and not on one of those fad diets where anything more than lettuce was banned.

He'd scrambled up some eggs with peppers, onions and tomatoes, topping it off with a scoop of his mom's homemade salsa while Maggie buttered toast and generally got in his way, but he hadn't minded—not at all.

The teasing touches and flirtatious rubs as they'd worked to prepare the meal had made him ravenous, but not for the food. Magdalena Holt was everything he liked in a woman; smart, funny, independent, and beautiful with her long, wavy black hair, almond-shaped eyes and vixen's body. He respected her. It wasn't easy to become an operator, and from all accounts she excelled at her job. Or had, until the Sinaloa Cartel got hold of her. It reminded him of the prisoners they'd rescued in Iraq—empty shells of the men they once were. The only way he could think of to pull her out of a downward spiral was to give her a reason to live. He'd like that reason to be him, but wasn't vain enough to think it was enough, even if he could get her to care about him. Maggie lived and breathed law enforcement. If he wanted her to be truly happy, he had to do whatever he could to get her reinstated with her team.

"Aren't you eating?" she asked, a triangle of jam-laden toast in hand.

Frank held up his beer. "Later. I bribed you so I wouldn't have to drink alone."

She licked cherry jam from her lips, stopping his heart. "And do you do that often?"

He folded his arms on the table to cover what she was doing to him down below and cleared his throat. "Do what?"

"Drink alone, silly." She chuckled and picked up her own drink.

He tapped the corner of his mouth. "You missed a spot —here."

Her eyes widened as a heated awareness flared between them. She rubbed at the jam and it came away on her finger.

Giving in to impulse, Frank snagged her hand before she could clean it off. "Let me," he said, his voice a low rumble, and gently sucked the sweetness from her skin. "Mmm, good."

"Frank," she whispered, her gaze on his lips. "Not a good idea."

"Really?" he asked, working his way down to her palm. "Why not?" He gave her hand a last, lingering kiss and closed her fingers around it before reluctantly letting go. "Don't worry, princess, I won't do anything you don't want me to. But," he added, holding her bemused gaze, "I'm putting you on notice. I like you, Magdalena. A lot. And I want a chance with you, if you'll let me."

She looked down at the fingers she was mangling in her lap. "I... like you, too, but—"

He shook his head, stopping her from shooting a hole in his heart. "Don't say it. I shouldn't have opened my big mouth—ignore me." He took a fortifying chug of beer and sought to change the subject. "So, how about those Dallas Cowboys?"

Maggie burst out laughing and it was the sweetest sound he'd heard in a long time. She took his hand and his pulse buzzed in his ears so that he almost missed what she was saying.

"—surprised you like football? You strike me as more of a tennis type. I bet you'd rock a pair of white shorts." He lost himself in the mischievous sparkle of her beautiful cinnamon eyes.

"That's the way you want to play, is it? I'll have you know we won a blue ribbon the year I was captain of my elementary school tennis team."

She snorted, the sound incongruous coming from that delicate nose. She clapped a hand over her mouth, snickering. "I bet you were adorable as a kid."

Not so sure adorable was the right adjective. More like competitive. He'd always had a drive to be the best, sometimes to his own detriment.

"Nah, that was my younger brother, Cam. He was the charmer."

Maggie stared at him with observant eyes. "Was? Sounds as though there's a story there—want to talk about it?"

Frank shrugged, sorry he'd brought Cameron up. "Not much to say. I wasn't there when he needed me, and now he's gone, end of story."

An uncomfortable silence—the first one of the night—fell between them and he cursed under his breath. "I'm sorry, it's just that Cam is a sore subject in this household. Mom insists it wasn't my fault, but I tend to look at things differently. I knew he was getting bullied and I should have done something about it. Instead, I told him to grow a set, can you believe that?" He scowled and stared out the darkened window. "Not quite so adorable now, huh?"

"I think you're being too hard on yourself," Maggie said quietly. "You were trying to toughen up your younger brother—to protect him from the bullies of the world. That's admirable, Frank."

He turned to her, doubtfully. "Why do I feel like a class-

A asshole, then?" She looked so earnest, trying to convince him of an integrity he didn't have.

"An asshole is someone who goes out of their way to make another person miserable—to degrade and humiliate. That's not you, it could never be you. Whatever happened with your brother wasn't your responsibility. You were a kid too, I presume?"

"Yeah," he said grudgingly, "ninth grade."

"Well then, you couldn't possibly know what he was going through. Sensitive children often bear the brunt of cruel tormenters, especially at that age. And there are animals who will take advantage of their distress by promising them a better life, anything their hearts desire—"

"You're talking about human traffickers." Frank's stomach roiled.

Maggie nodded, her expression grave. "It's a possibility, I'm afraid. I've done some background work on your brother, as I promised, and the trail goes cold in Austin. No body and no recent witnesses. The last person to see Cameron was a bus driver who remembers a guy in a business suit talking to him shortly after he disembarked, a red backpack over one shoulder. Police later found the bag in the hands of a home-less man with no idea of how he came to have it on his person. But then, you know this. You tracked that homeless man down, fed him and gave him a place to stay, didn't you?"

"He belonged to someone—had a mother, father, siblings, maybe even a wife and children," Frank said simply.

"I couldn't get much personal information out of him. I keep hoping and praying Cam was treated to the same courtesy, even if he couldn't bring himself to call us for help."

"You're a good man, Frank Stein." Maggie surprised him with tears.

"Don't cry for me, Maggie Mae, I don't deserve it. There's way too much anger in my heart." He rose and circled the table to pull her into his arms and closed his eyes, the better to take in all the sensations bombarding his senses. She fit perfectly with his chin resting on her fragrant hair and her cheek nestled against his heart. He could have stayed that way all night.

Or until Adam interrupted them. "Mag's, there you..."

Maggie jerked in his arms, as though she'd stepped into another zone and had been yanked back by her partner's voice. She looked up at him with something like regret in her star-bright eyes before backing away, wiping surreptitiously at the tears on her lashes.

"Were you looking for me?" she asked Adam as she gathered her dishes and carried them to the sink.

Frank crossed his empty arms, trying, and failing, not to resent the interruption.

"I thought you were tired?" Adam accused, a dark frown marring his face.

"I persuaded her to keep me company for a while. You got a problem with that?" Frank growled.

"As a matter of..."

"Stop it. You two are acting like schoolyard bullies—" The moment the words left her lips, Frank could see her desperately trying to reel them back in. She looked at him with a plea for understanding before turning to Adam. "Last time I checked, I was a grown woman. Now, if there's nothing more important, I will bid you gentlemen goodnight."

She strode to the doorway with her chin in the air, black hair bouncing with every step. "Thanks for the eggs, Frank, they were delicious."

He gave a slight nod, for some reason amused by the tongue-lashing they'd received. "Goodnight, Maggie Mae. Sweet dreams."

She flushed and hurried from the room and he would have been tempted to give away his finest horseflesh to know what those dreams would be.

"Are you getting hooked on Maggie?" Adam asked, his tone disbelieving.

Frank scowled. "And what if I am?" He didn't want to fight his buddy, but all bets were off when it came to Magdalena. She was under his skin and he didn't plan on letting go.

"Be careful, man. She's special."

Yeah, she was. Probably too good for either of them, but that wasn't going to stop him from trying to win her heart.

I t was mid-afternoon by the time Nick dropped Jack
off at his vehicle and drove home with Jenny and her
dogs. Sara hadn't been thrilled with the prospect of his
ex-girlfriend in their home, never mind two Rottweilers, but
she'd agreed it was for the best once he explained about the
break-in. He'd withheld the news of the missing convicts,
reluctant to worry her needlessly. Besides, it was doubtful
the men would risk entering the township unless they
became desperate.

"Thanks again, Nick. I really wasn't looking forward to
staying in the house alone tonight." Jenny smiled shakily.

Their little three-bedroom house was already filled to
overflowing with Jared's kids. He wasn't sure where they
would place Jenny, but they'd figure something out.

He pulled into the asphalt driveway and parked. "It's no

problem. Shall we go in?" He was anxious to hold his wife and children and assure himself of their safety.

Jenny glanced into the backseat. "What about Bonnie and Clyde?"

Nick turned in his seat to see the dogs panting and staring at them with hungry eyes. He chuckled. "I think we better get them fed."

The door opened and Sara stood in the entry, Caleb on her hip. As it had since the first moment he saw her, Nick's pulse raced. Except now, along with the attraction, there was a deep-seated tenderness and abiding love for the woman who'd gifted him with her trust and adoration after the abuse she'd endured with her first husband.

"Da, da. Da, da," Caleb called, arms out and chubby fingers stretched as though he could reach his father through willpower alone.

Nick grinned and opened the car door. One leg was already out when he was reminded of his company.

"You're a lucky man," Jenny murmured.

He nodded. "I know. Come and meet my son."

Leaving her to follow at her own pace, he hurried forward and wrapped his family in his arms. Kissing the top of Caleb's downy head, he turned and caught his wife's pursed lips. They immediately softened, letting him in on a sigh.

"I'm glad you're home," she whispered.

"Me too," he agreed. "I missed you."

"Mith you," Caleb parroted, his gummy grin squeezing Nick's heart.

He leaned back and opened his arms for his son. "Come here, little man. Give Mommy a break. You're getting to be such a big boy."

Caleb latched on like a leech, his stubby arms choking, though Nick didn't mind a bit. "Big boy," he echoed, though it came out in gibberish. Then he caught sight of Jenny and her dogs over his dad's shoulder. "Woof, woof," he squealed, his little body stiff with excitement.

Sara raised a brow before turning to their guest with a welcoming smile. "Hello, Jenny. Please, come in. Are your dogs good with children? I'm afraid we have a houseful at the moment."

Jenny had stopped halfway up the drive, the flirtatious smile she normally wore nowhere in sight. Instead, she looked at Nick's family unit with something like envy, her gaze warm as it rested on the baby. "Bonnie and Clyde love kids. I often take them to work with me to acclimate them to different sounds. They're very well behaved, truly."

"Okay, then," Sara said, standing aside so they could enter the house. "I'm sure you remember Nick's dog, Jake. He's not here right now," she glanced back at Nick, "Jess and Chris took him for a walk while the baby went down for a nap. He's protective of the children, so you might want to keep the dogs separated when they're around."

Nick looked at the darkening sky with some misgiving.

"When did they leave? It's getting kind of late, isn't it?" He was probably overreacting, but with criminals on the loose...

"They should be back soon. They were going to the park for a while. Don't worry, Jessica is responsible."

Yeah, she was, but that didn't stop his gut from telling him something was wrong. He'd give them another half hour and then call to see if they were on their way. He gave Jenny an absent smile. "Would you like to see your room first, or join us for coffee?"

"You men and your coffee," Sara said, sending him a chastising glance. "I just made a fresh pot of chai tea, Jenny—unless you prefer coffee?"

"No, no. Tea sounds lovely, thank you. Please don't go to any bother for me. I can sleep on your sofa. I don't want to displace anyone." Jenny followed them into the house, keeping a tight hold on her dogs' leashes. "I would like to get these two fed though, if that's all right? I'm afraid with all the excitement, they didn't have their morning meal."

Nick held out his hand for the leashes. "I'll settle them in while you and Sara get reacquainted. We have a kennel set up in the backyard, they'll be safe enough there." He passed Caleb over to his mother. "You stay here with Mom, little man. I'll be right back." Sara's gaze warned him he'd better be. He grinned and kissed her. "Keep my *tea* warm, honey."

Leaving the women to sort themselves out, he escaped into their fenced yard with the dogs in tow. The large cherry tree was covered in buds and would soon be giving them a show with its multitude of pink flowers, but for now its bare branches stretched skeletal fingers across the lawn. He stepped off the deck they frequently used during barbeque season, just as the wind kicked up, sending the swing set he'd built for Jessica creaking and groaning like an old woman. It reminded him he needed to grease the joints and retorque the screws before Caleb used it.

"Okay, you two, here's your new temporary digs. Jake's left his scent everywhere back here, so it'll give you a chance to get used to him before there's an actual meet-and-greet. Play nice, the old boy's been through hell and back with me. He deserves your respect." Bonnie and Clyde stared at him with intelligent eyes as though they understood every word. They probably did. Animals were a lot smarter than humans gave them credit for. If it wasn't for Jake's quick reflexes and superior senses, he'd be dead right now.

He filled their food dishes from the bins he kept in the shed attached to the kennel and topped up the water bowl from the outside tap, made sure the cage was secure, then headed back to the house, rubbing his hands against the chill.

"Whew, that wind is cold," he said, wrapping his hands around the mug Sara set before him. "It's going to be a nippy night, I'm afraid." He gazed apologetically at Jenny, who was looking decidedly spent. "Will they be okay outside?" He felt bad, but he didn't know her animals and didn't trust them wandering the house at night.

"Bonnie and Clyde spend more time outdoors than they

do inside, they'll settle better out there." She yawned and blushed, covering her mouth. "I'm so sorry. I didn't get much sleep last night, what with—"

"We understand," Nick hurried to assure her in case she'd been about to mention the men she'd seen. "Sara will take you to your room and we can talk in the morning."

Sara had already risen, her hand on Nick's shoulder. "I've prepared Jessica's bedroom for you, she can bunk down with her brother."

"Are they home then?" Nick asked. "I haven't seen them."

Sara's brow furrowed as she glanced out the window. "No. They should have been here a while ago. Can you call Jess while I get Jenny settled in?"

Nick nodded, already pulling his phone from his pocket. That uneasy feeling was back, and he rubbed his gut as he dialed.

Ring.

Ring.

Ring.

"This is Jess. I'm too busy to talk right now. Leave a message and I'll call you back, I promise."

Frowning, he hung up and tried three more times before finally leaving a message. "This is your Dad. Call me." He ended the call and stood to pace to the window. Maybe he should take a drive by the park, just to...

"Nick. Oh, my God, Nick, they're gone." Sara rushed

into the room with Jenny on her heels. She swayed on her feet and Nick hurried to grasp her arms before she fell.

"Who's gone?" he demanded, dread a leaden ball in his stomach.

"J... Jess and Chris. She left a note on her dresser and her backpack is missing." Tears hovered on her lashes. "Why didn't I notice the note, Nick? Why?"

He took her trembling body in his arms, knowing she was reliving those horrible days when the kids had been kidnapped by a man bent on revenge against Jared.

Jenny stared at them with empathy shining from her eyes. "Could it be...?

Nick shook his head violently, staving off the words. "They're just running late. Probably goofing around and didn't realize how late it was getting, that's all. Calm down, love. Let's not jump to conclusions."

"But, the note," she cried, staring up at him with genuine fear.

"What note?" he asked, even as Jenny held out a piece of paper ripped from a scribbler. He accepted it with numb fingers. Jessica's distinctive left-hand cursive mocked his attempted denial of a danger he'd sensed for much of the day.

Don't be mad.
Chris and I decided to go camping

Without you.
We're old enough,
And want to prove ourselves.
Don't worry,
Jake is with us.
We know what to do,
After all,
You taught us well.
Jess

NICK'S HEART plummeted to his toes and he broke out in a cold sweat. This was his fault. He'd promised them a camping trip and reneged. Jessica was headstrong and independent, just like her mom. She'd taken her hurt feelings and done something about it. If he wasn't so frightened, he'd applaud her initiative. After he grounded her for life.

He looked into his wife's beautiful brown eyes and kissed her, trying to instill the strength she would need to get through the next few hours. "I'll find them, honey, I promise, okay?" He waited until she gave him a faint nod. "I'm going to head out and check a few places. Can you call Jared? Let him know what's happened, and that we'll keep them updated."

He lifted his head and met Jenny's gaze. "Phone the

sheriff and fill him in, would you? Tell him I'm heading out to the Pinedale Campground. He can meet me there."

"Of course. I'll keep Sara company until you get back," she said.

With, or without, the children.

Nick clenched his jaw and strode for the door. He wouldn't give up until he found them.

21

Frank met up with his employees the next morning and warned them to keep their eyes open while out in the fields.

"I saw a few shot up signs on the south access road the other day and more fencing down. Could be a coincidence, or it could be those rustlers we've been having trouble with." Or the drug runners the DEA were after, but he kept that to himself. Most of the men had families and it was his responsibility to make sure they arrived home safe and sound every night.

"Another week and we should have most of the calves branded, then we can move them into the summer grazing pastures. How are the Santa Gertrudis yearlings looking, Spencer? I have a big sale planned for the middle of next month." Frank leaned on the paddock rails and watched his mares and colts out in the field.

"They're looking good, boss. Should bring top dollar, no problem."

"I want a count done on the herd. I have a feeling we're going to come up short, and if that's true, I need to know about it." All the ranches in the area had been plagued off and on for months now by cattle rustlers and it was seriously pissing him off. He'd managed—with Adam and Amanda's help—to take down one of the poachers a couple of months ago, but the guy had clammed up and hired an expensive lawyer.

Moody gray clouds crept over the horizon, adding to his surly attitude. It felt as though even Mother Nature was conspiring against him. He'd thought inviting Maggie to his ranch would give her a chance to rest and restore herself, instead he'd thrown her headlong into the whirlpool that was his life. He wouldn't be surprised if she grabbed the first plane out.

"Something you want to talk about?" Spencer asked as the men went about their duties.

Frank glanced over his shoulder. "I thought I just did."

Spence frowned and shoved a wad of gum in his mouth. "Your mother wants me to quit chewing tobacco, it's making me cranky, too."

"About time, and I'm not *cranky*."

"Coulda fooled me," Spence grumbled. "You wear your heart on your sleeve, you always have. The ranch is like the land, son, enduring. It was here long before you and it'll be here for future generations after we're dead and gone. But that lady of yours, she's the one who needs you now. You should be concentrating on *that* problem, leave us to care for your cows."

Frank shook his head in amazement. "I think that's the longest speech I've ever heard you give, you old coot. Love is turning you soft."

"Pshaw," Spencer growled, but his eyes glowed and a smile split his lips. "And even if it is, you could learn something from it. You've put in your time, Frank. Grab for the moon before it's gone." He slapped his hat against his thigh, clamped it down on his gray head, and strode toward the barn, Mom's dog, Sugar, at his heels.

Frank swore and then chuckled. Spencer Tate, philosopher—it kind of had a ring to it. And speaking of rings... that was another conversation he needed to be having with his manager. If Spence was serious about his mom, he'd better make an honest woman of her. Maybe that was old-fashioned opinions in this day and age, but he'd been brought up to respect women, and to his way of thinking, asking for their hand in marriage was the ultimate sign of respect. It meant you were willing to forgo all others and promise to love, cherish, and protect them for the rest of their life. So, yeah, a ring was a big deal.

And why he was thinking about life and love? Damn that Spencer.

Disgusted, he stomped across the concourse and

entered the pen with his new stallion, Desert Dancer. Luke Farthing, a state champion bronc rider, was working the spirited animal in the center of the ring and, like the pro he was, ignored the distraction, keeping his focus where it should be, on those powerful hooves and expressive eyes.

The animal was mesmerizing and knew it. He kept his head up high, nostrils quivering as he picked up the scents around him. He didn't pace so much as prance, the high, springy steps reminiscent of the Lipizzaner horses in his ancestry. Spanish, Arabian, and Berber blood had created a magnificent piece of horseflesh valued in racing and dressage alike. Frank was lucky to have had the opportunity to purchase an animal with Desert Dancer's lineage. It should guarantee him top dollar stud fees, as well as the chance to build an impressive herd of his own. It all depended on the stallion. While his feisty nature might be a turn-on for the ladies, he also needed to be well-mannered for the gents—hence today's exercise.

"How's he doing?" Frank called out, pleased to see that other than a quiver down his flank, Dancer didn't seem bothered by the noise.

"Coming along," Luke said, turning slowly in time with the horse's wider loop. "He's a beaut. Don't think I've seen a finer animal in all my years on the circuit."

Frank nodded, his gaze transfixed on the smooth flow of muscle under a dove gray coat. "Just watch him. He likes to nip if you aren't paying attention. Wrecked one of my good shirts last week."

"A horse managed to get the drop on the infamous SEAL Team Five's Senior Chief? I find that hard to believe."

Maggie's amused voice set Frank's pulse thundering twice as loud as Desert Dancer's hooves. He turned to see her sitting on the top rail, slender legs encased in faded jeans, one leg ripped at the knee, and red heels on her feet.

"Those shoes—" He jerked his gaze up to her face. She looked like his wildest fantasy in that getup.

She grinned and held out a foot, turning a shapely ankle this way and that. "I know, right? I bought them just before..." The smile did a downward slide. "Anyway, today's the day."

"They're eye-catching, if inappropriate for farm work." That flash of despair made his chest hurt.

"Good thing I'm just watching then, isn't it?" she quipped, obviously making an effort to restore her good mood. She shifted her gaze to the center of the ring. "He doesn't look very happy."

Frank strode over and rested his arm on the rail near her thigh, telling himself it was so they could converse more quietly and not stress the stallion, but his heart knew better.

"It's a battle of wills. Dancer knows what he needs to do, but he doesn't plan on making it too easy on us. It's all part of breaking a horse."

"Breaking? No wonder he's fighting you." Fingers with

nails as red as her heels gripped the fence, leaving half-moon imprints in the rough wood.

He looked from her to the spirited animal in the ring and cursed under his breath. The similarities between what they were doing and what Chenglei had attempted with Maggie became glaringly apparent.

"Farthing," he snapped. "That's enough for today. Cool him down and set him out to pasture, we'll try again tomorrow."

Luke nodded and relaxed his hold on the bullwhip he'd been using behind Dancer's haunches to keep him moving the way he wanted. "Sure thing, boss, whatever you say."

Frank waited until Farthing led the lightly sweating stallion out of the enclosure before trying to explain a practice that might seem cruel, but actually didn't hurt the animal at all.

He placed a hand on Maggie's knee, calming her nervous jittering. "Breaking is just a term, my men would never harm an animal on the ranch."

She looked down at him, her eyes unbearably sad. "Do you think it's fair to harness someone weaker than yourself and enforce your will on them?"

He frowned. "Of course not. What do you take me for?"

She slid her hand under his and threaded their fingers together. "Isn't that what you're doing to the horse?"

No. But he could see where she might think so and it

bothered him. "You're on my ranch for a week and already you want to change things, huh?"

She peeked at him from under dark lashes. "Are you angry?"

This time he said it aloud. "No. Hell, no. Just because something is done by rote, doesn't make it right. I'll have a talk with Farthing. We'll figure out a new training method and see how it goes."

"Really?" she asked, her eyes sparkling.

"Really," he agreed. His chest swelled in tempo with her excitement.

"You're okay, you know that?" She gifted him with a radiant smile and an impulsive hug.

Frank stilled, overwhelmed by the thrill of having her in his arms. Then, slowly, carefully, he returned the embrace, soaking up the vanilla-sweet scent of her hair and the silky softness of her neck.

All too soon, it ended.

Maggie released her hold and leaned back, breaking his grip. "That was..."

"Nice," he finished. Incredible. Life-altering. Mind-blowing. Just a few of the adjectives that came to mind. Instead, he went with the most boring word on the planet —geez.

"Nice," she agreed, softly. "On the upside, I didn't knee you in the nuts and run screaming for the hills. I'd say that's a plus."

Frank sputtered a shocked laugh, even as his balls ducked and rolled—metamorphically speaking, at least. "I'm glad you restrained yourself," he chuckled, wiping wet eyes. "I'd hate having to explain *that* to the men."

Maggie smirked and hopped down from the fence, landing like a cat on those toothpicks she called shoes. "Don't underestimate me, Chief. I'm tougher than I look."

If there was one thing he was sure of, it was this woman's innate strength. What she'd been through would destroy most men, and yet, here she was, a phoenix rising from the ashes of her past. He should be bowing at her feet.

"Good. I have stalls that need cleaning," he said, counting himself a lucky bastard to receive the gift of her smiles. He wanted to wake up every morning with Maggie at his side. To marry her, raise children, and grow old together right here on the healing spirit of the ranch—if she'd have him. He'd scoffed at tales of love at first sight, but he wasn't mocking those people anymore. Maggie had embedded herself in his heart way back in a Las Vegas interrogation room, and he'd been chasing her affections ever since. But now, their time had arrived.

"Tell you what, I'll supervise," she murmured, wrinkling her nose at the substantial manure pile stacked to the side of the barn.

"City girl." He chuckled. "I'll make you a deal. You—"

"Something's wrong," she interrupted, raising her arm as Jared and Adam burst from the barn, their expressions grim.

That ugly premonition rose again, curdling the pleasure in Frank's chest. Apparently, fun time had come to an end. He and Maggie crossed the yard to meet them, each step like a quicksand he couldn't escape.

"It's Chris," Jared blurted, his eyes devastated. "He and Sara got this crazy idea to go camping on their own and now they're missing and I'm in the middle of fricking nowheresville. Sorry, man," he added, meeting Frank's gaze. "It's just that by the time we get to an airport..."

Frank shook his head. "No need to apologize. Have you called the police? Of course, you have. Nick's a good man, I'm sure he's already got feet on the ground. Try to stay calm, okay? I have a couple of rancher friends with biplanes. I'll give them a call, maybe someone can expedite your trip."

Jared clasped his arm. "Thanks, Chief. It's just, after last time... And if that's not bad enough, apparently there are a couple of escaped convicts in the area." His laugh was harsh, frightened. "When it rains, it fucking pours, right?"

Talk about having the past rear up and bite you on the ass. "They're smart kids. Stay positive, okay? I'll call in a few favors and see if we can't get some infrared maps of the area. Give me a couple of hours to line something up and I'll follow you as soon I can." He'd been there when a Russian hitman kidnapped the kids to get to Jared. It had been shortly after his buddy found out he was the father of an eight-year-old. And then, to nearly lose him... it almost killed Jared—and Annie, too.

He glanced at a worried Maggie. "Will you and your team be okay here?" Damn, he hated to leave them, but Jared was his brother-at-arms, he had to go. "Just don't do anything rash until I get back, it'll only be a day or two." He hoped.

Adam stepped forward and shook his hand, then gave Jared a man-hug. "Call if there's anything we can do on our end. Keep the faith, you'll find them."

They had to.

22

Maggie waited with Frank's mom on the front porch while he loaded gear into the heavy-duty truck he'd used to pick them up from the airport. This time, he was getting ready to fly out and support another friend. He seemed to step in whenever he was needed. She wondered who helped him when he needed it?

"That boy has the biggest heart," his mom said, their thoughts eerily similar. She glanced sideways at Maggie before redirecting her attention to her son. "Ever since he was a child, Frank took it upon himself to be the caretaker for his family. He took his duties seriously, too." Her smile was soft. "Made sure his brother never got into trouble, even though it seemed to follow Cameron wherever he went."

They watched as he opened the hood and tinkered with

the motor, then wiped his hands with a rag before letting the cover drop with a bang.

"It tore him up something fierce when his father died. Frank was supposed to go with him that day, but he'd been feeling under the weather, so I made him stay home. Then the storm kicked up and Frank knew—deep in his gut—that his daddy was hurt." She jabbed her hands deep in the pockets of her wool sweater and sat in the rocking chair as though her legs were too weak to hold her up. "By the time Spencer and some of the other men found him, it was too late, he was gone." She shook her head and stared at the horizon. "This can be an unforgiving land if you're not careful. I've laid my mother, father and husband to rest here. One day it will take me, too." She turned to Maggie. "I want to see my sons happy before that happens."

Maggie didn't know what to say. Emily Stein had lived through tremendous losses yet still maintained a gracious dignity that was admirable. It had to be incredibly hard to let Frank go on his missions with the SEALs, to never know if the next time she saw her child he'd be alive, or in a pine box with his country's flag draped over the casket.

"How do you do it?" she asked, not sure she'd have the strength to sit by while her loved ones rushed into danger.

"Faith," Emily said, fingering the gold crucifix she wore around her neck. She smiled and patted the seat of the rocker next to hers. "Frank's father gave me this on our wedding day. It gives me comfort to know He watches over my boys, wherever they are."

That was the second time she'd referred to her younger son as though he were alive. Maggie couldn't imagine hanging onto hope for that many years without any contact. Unless...

She took the proffered seat and gently grasped the blue-veined hand. "Emily, have you heard from Cameron?"

Instead of being startled, Frank's mom nodded, and Maggie's heart took off to the races. She glanced out to the drive, debating whether to call him up to the house, but, before she could, Emily clarified her earthshattering statement.

"I see him in my dreams." Her gaze turned introspective, as though, with a little effort, she could conjure him up whenever she wanted—and maybe she could. "He's grown into a fine young man. Tall and handsome, just like his father."

Maggie had heard of recollective dream therapy, where patients work through their traumas by walking back in time. But she'd never heard of any cases where the subjects aged within the treatments. Was it possible Emily had the early stages of dementia? It would break Frank's heart if that were true. He was so close to his mom, it was a joy to witness.

Hoping to humor her until Frank joined them, she delved deeper into Emily's dreams. "What is Cameron doing when you... see him?"

She frowned and squinted as though trying to break through the veils of time. "I'm not sure... traveling maybe? Sometimes, he's on an airplane, at other times he's driving, but I can't tell where. He never lets me see out the windows, I'm not sure why." She rubbed her brow and let her hand fall to her lap. "You probably think I'm crazy."

Maggie slipped to the floor so she could be closer and offer comfort. "My momma believed the spirits of those who are gone live on until we're ready to say goodbye. Maybe your son knows you aren't there yet." She rested her hand over Emily's and smiled.

"What's going on here?" Frank asked, climbing the stairs to join them on the porch. He bent over to kiss his mom's cheek before giving Maggie a questioning glance. "Everything okay?"

Maggie squeezed Emily's hand and rose, feeling at a distinct disadvantage on the floor at this man's feet. "Sure. We were getting better acquainted, right, Emily?" She didn't want to worry him about his mother just before he left. They could talk when he returned.

Emily nodded and blinked up at Frank. "I was just telling your young lady about my dreams of Cameron. I don't think she believed me, but she was very gracious."

Maggie's heart plummeted. She wasn't sure which was worse, Emily's misconceptions about her and Frank's relationship, or her embarrassment at getting called out by such a sweet lady.

"I'm so sorry, I didn't mean—"

"Don't worry about it," Frank interrupted her awkward apology. He took the seat she'd vacated and leaned on the arm of his mother's rocking chair. "Momma, did you have another vision?"

Vision? Maggie shivered and wrapped her arms around herself to control the trembling that overtook her limbs. She'd had strange, psychosis-type dreams out in the desert after her escape from Chenglei's henchmen and had put them down to dehydration and the fever she'd been running after getting shot. Yet, those dreams had guided her steps out of that hellhole. She was ashamed of herself for doubting Frank's mom.

Emily used an embroidered hankie to dab at the tears leaking from the corners of her eyes. "More often lately. He's reaching out to us, Franco, I know he is."

Frank looked at Maggie, his expression strained. "Could you get Mom a glass of water, please?"

"Of course. I'll be right back." She opened the door and hesitated on the threshold, glancing back at mother and son, their dark heads bent together, nearly touching. Her throat tightened. It had been so long since she'd had moments like that with her own mother, it was bittersweet to witness Frank's devotion to his parent. She was falling for the big cowboy and wished she had her mom to talk to. The mental and physical abuse she'd suffered as Chenglei's prisoner had scarred her for life. She didn't know if it would ever be possible to have a normal relationship with a man, and it wasn't fair to let them think she could. It would be better to back away from Frank now, before it was too late.

Heart heavy, she strode into the kitchen and gasped, surprising Amanda and Adam in a torrid embrace. They jumped away from each other like scalded cats, Adam the epitome of frustrated male, and Amanda with her chin in the air. *"Nothing to see here, folks."*

"I'm so sorry," Maggie babbled, not sure where to put her eyes. "I was just getting Emily a glass of water. It's warm outside and she was thirsty, and Frank—"

"It's okay, Mags, forget it. I was leaving anyway. I know when I'm not wanted." Adam sent Amanda a fuming glare and strode out the back door, letting the screen slam shut.

Amanda scowled, then sagged like a balloon losing air. "I suppose you want an explanation." She touched her swollen lips and sighed. "I'm not trying to steal your man, if that's what you're thinking."

Maggie stared, disconcerted. Did she mean Adam? "Adam and I are friends and partners, nothing more."

Amanda gave her the side-eye. "Come on, Holt, I know you two were hot and heavy for a while. I only let it go because it didn't seem to affect your performance on the job. He was distraught when you were abducted. You can't tell me he doesn't have feelings for you."

Wow, SAC Rhinehold and Adam. She hadn't seen that one coming. Though truthfully, they made sense. Amanda could use a little lightening up, and Adam... well, he was as loyal as they came. Just because she couldn't see herself in a relationship, it didn't mean her best friend couldn't find true love—and she was going to help him.

"If you care about him at all, give Adam a chance. He's worth it, Amanda." She moved to the sink and ran the water, giving the other woman a moment to digest what she'd said. "I would still be in that desert if not for Adam's determination. I will love him forever, but I'm not *in* love with him, okay?"

When Amanda didn't answer, she turned and almost dropped the glass she was holding. Frank stood in the doorway, and the flame in his eyes heated her from the inside out.

"Well okay, then," he murmured, with one of those rare, heart-stopping smiles. "Now, we're getting somewhere."

23

Brian walked down his family's drive, nursing a throbbing head and sore shoulder where he'd taken a random hit with a pool cue at the bar Friday night. He didn't know where Lennox or Jenkins ended up and couldn't care less—he was done with those two.

The call he'd been expecting came in. Grimacing, he tugged the phone out of his back pocket. Unknown number. No surprise there. Rivero was a master at covering his tracks. If he ever discovered who'd narced out and got him arrested, they'd be dead.

He tapped the call button. "Yeah."

"Is that any way to answer the phone, *mi amigo*?"

The voice from his nightmares sent a chill up Brian's spine. "We aren't friends. What do you want, Rivero?"

"Careful. I might decide I miss my roomie." His chuckle was low and wicked.

Brian scowled at a pair of deer that wandered out of the woods and stared at him before bounding away. Their freedom wasn't lost on him. "I'm keeping my nose clean. I ain't going back in. You'll have to put a hit out on me."

"Don't tempt me," Rivero snapped, the jocular tone gone. "I heard all about your very public night out. Is that what you're there for?"

Brian stared at the black face of his phone and shook his head. How the hell...? Jenkins, it had to be. He hated Lennox but knew him for the scum that he was. Jenkins made him nervous. The man had sharp eyes. He was a wild card, and Brian didn't like the odds.

"You're preachin' to the choir, man. Tell those other idiots. I was only there to keep the peace."

"Don't worry, it won't be happening again. You screw this deal up for me and there won't be a rock big enough to hide your skinny white ass under—you feel me?"

Even from prison, Rivero had the ability to turn him into a sniveling coward. He'd had the man's protection in jail, but the price... never again.

"I get it. How much longer?" He kicked a hapless bush alongside the road and almost went down, his foot catching in the branches. He fumbled the phone, and for a brief instant considered letting it crash to the ground. With any luck it would break, and he wouldn't have to talk to the prick anymore. Unfortunately, the possible repercussions raised their ugly heads, and he made the save in time to catch the tail end of Rivero's pronouncement.

"—weekend, be ready."

Shit. The only useful piece of the conversation and he'd missed it. He'd have to pump Lennox and Jenkins, there was no way he was asking Rivero to repeat himself.

A vehicle turned off the cut-across road between his property and Bella Vista. Brian squinted but he couldn't tell who was about to pay them an impromptu visit. Time to wrap up this joyful reunion.

"We'll have everything organized. Should go off without a hitch. Just remember, this is it. After our job is completed, I want out, like we agreed." He hated the pleading tone but couldn't control the very real fear that Rivero would never let him go.

"Do you question my word? Do the work, *mi amigo,* then we talk." The background noise of other inmates placing calls on the bank of phones set out for their use died, leaving an ominous foreboding in Brian's gut. He should have known it wasn't going to be that easy. Rivero had claimed him, and he wasn't a man to let his possessions go. Maybe he should just kill himself and get it over with. At least then he'd be leaving on his own terms.

The vehicle morphed into the nondescript gray sedan Jenkins drove. Brian thought briefly of jumping the fence and sprinting into the woods, never to be seen again, but it was too late, he'd been spotted.

The car covered the intervening distance, then slowed to a stop. The smoked glass window on the driver's side whispered down and Jenkins stared at him from behind a pair of dark sunglasses. "Going somewhere?"

Brian suppressed the urge to tell him to get lost. This was the first time he'd seen the other man without his sidekick—he planned to take advantage of it.

"Walking into town for breakfast—interested?"

Jenkins took his sweet time answering, as though mulling over every syllable for hidden meanings, before he shrugged and said, "Get in."

Shoving his hands deep into his pockets, Brian circled the car and climbed in on the passenger side. He was about to either do something incredibly stupid or make the smartest decision of his twenty-five years on God's green earth.

"I know who you are," he said, and was rewarded with jerk on the steering wheel.

Jenkins straightened out and slid him a sharp sideways glance. "What the hell, man. You been watching them horror movies again? Cheesy dialogue aside, you should warn a guy before making those kinds of statements."

Riding a wave of satisfaction, Brian stretched his legs and smirked. "You gave yourself away the other night, just so's you know. Any self-respecting criminal would have celebrated the chance to break bottles over some heads. Not you though. You dove out of the Pickled Pepper like your pants were on fire. Why is that I asked myself? You want to know what I came up with?"

He had to give the man credit. Other than the one slip, there was no way to figure out if he was getting to him. Jenkins drove casually, one arm bent on the open windowsill, the breeze carrying the scents of bluebonnets and mountain laurel mixed with dust from the road and dung from the cattle grazing in the field.

"My heart's all aflutter," the big man said. "Do tell."

Brian swallowed hard. After this, there was no going back. "You're a Fed, ain't ya?"

Jenkins turned those mirrored sunglasses in his direction, and he squirmed like a bug under a telescope. "Those are words that could get you killed. Are you sure you want to say them?"

Hell, no. He wasn't sure of anything other than his desperation to get out from under Rivero's thumb. "Look, it makes no never mind to me. You could be the president for all I care. I just thought we could maybe make a deal. You know, I give you something and you give me something back?"

Jenkins flipped on his blinker and turned. "And what is it you think I want, Finch?"

Brian glanced out the window and realized they weren't going to town. Instead, they were heading to an old flour mill on the banks of the Cypress River. His heart palpitated and his hands grew sweaty. He rubbed them absently on his jeans and looked for the best place to duck and roll while maintaining a pseudo-calm exterior.

"Well, it ain't breakfast, since you took a wrong turn back there." He gave Jenkins a nervous smile while feeling along the edge of his seat for a weapon of some sort. Where was the tire iron when a guy needed one? "No worries. There's an open field up ahead, you can whip around and we'll be on our way."

"I don't think that's a good idea, do you?" Jenkins asked and flipped the locks on the doors. "This chat is better held in private—if you know what I mean?" His turn with the lame-assed grin.

Panicking now, Brian reached for the steering wheel and got an elbow to the face for his efforts. "Ow, you son of a…" he cried, cupping his bleeding mouth. "I think you broke my nose."

"Didn't anyone ever tell you it's bad manners to grab for things?" Jenkins geared down for the pothole-filled gravel road. "Now sit tight. I have someone I want you to meet."

Unable to do anything else, Brian flopped back in his seat and watched his life go down the tube.

24

Maggie squatted in the shadows of the dilapidated old building, her nerves jumping equally from the dubious state of the weathered roof over their heads and the meeting about to go down. With Frank gone, Amanda had stepped up her plans to stop the drug shipment into the country before the Renegade Resolvers used it to finance their rebellion.

She'd made a call and now, here they were, Adam, Amanda, and her crouched behind a pile of mildewy hay waiting for word from the FBI undercover operative that the job was a go. And that was another thing, when had Amanda planned on letting them know they were in bed with the Bureau on this op?

"We've been waiting for over an hour. Your guy's a no-show, my knees are killing me, and I think I have a hay allergy," Adam grumbled, starting to rise.

Amanda grabbed his arm and yanked him down. "We leave when I say we leave, and not before. He must have been held up. This location hasn't been breached so far, but I don't need one of my men blowing his cover, either. Now quit whining and keep your head down."

The line of Amanda's jaw betrayed the tense situation. Meeting with a snitch was always dicey, but it took on a whole *other* level of danger when the informer was an undercover agent. If his car was traced or he'd somehow been bugged, it could blow the entire operation, and probably get them all killed as a bonus.

"How well do you know this guy?" Maggie cursed under her breath. They definitely should have been forewarned of the threat to their safety *before* they left on this little jaunt.

Amanda shrugged, her gaze trained on a slowly growing dust cloud in the distance. "As well as can be expected considering the circumstances. He's supposedly one of their best and has built quite the reputation as a maverick in the organization. That's not to say I trust him as far as I can throw him—which as you will soon see, isn't very damn far. He's here," she added unnecessarily as a dirty gray sedan appeared, the sun glinting sharply off the windshield.

Curiosity warred with caution as the vehicle rolled to a stop a few feet from the gaping door of their negligible sanctuary. Maggie had worked with FBI agents a few times in her career and always found them to be circumspect to the point of being staid in their dark suits and thin ties. How that translated when undercover was anyone's guess.

A tall man with overlong sandy brown hair exited the car from the driver's side. He stood behind the open door for a few moments while he carefully inspected the perimeter. At least he was smart enough to assess the risks before opening himself up to a possible ambush.

Amanda rose, hand resting on her sidearm, and moved to where he could see her. "You're late," she called out.

He took a last look around and paced to the front of the car, his body coiled for a quick getaway. "Had a slight change of plan." He jerked his head back toward the passenger side of the vehicle. "I brought someone you should meet."

Amanda tensed and drew her gun. Adam cursed viciously and drew his, as well. "I'm going to slide along the wall, try and get a bead on the unsub. You stay here and back her up, okay?"

Maggie nodded, her ears hot and palms sweating. She unholstered the Glock 19 and took aim, grateful her hands were steady even though her nerves were singing.

"That's not how this works," Amanda said, her voice commanding attention. "You, out of the car, hands on the roof." She waved her gun to illustrate what she wanted. "I'm disappointed, Jenkins. I thought we had an understanding."

He frowned and shook his head, his gaze unerringly tracking Maggie's gun though she rested her arm on the scratchy hay bale in the gloomy shadows of the old building.

"Looks like we're both disappointed then." He held his hands out to show no weapons, at least none they could see. "Are we done playing cops and robbers? I don't have all day."

Another man, this one younger, with dark, floppy hair and a slim build had climbed from the car while he was talking and took position, hands on roof, feet spread, as though he'd done it many times before. No doubt he had.

"Who's your date?" Amanda asked, nodding for Adam to pat both men down.

Maggie held her breath, her finger itching to squeeze the trigger. When had she become this shoot now, ask questions later, agent? She didn't like it. Her reaction should be cautionary, but not violent, and going by the blood boiling through her veins at the moment, the FBI was in danger of losing one of their finest. She snorted, relieving some of the tension, and eased her finger a hairsbreadth from the trigger.

"His name is Finch. Brian Finch. He has property near here. The organization we're both interested in recruited him in prison." The Fed turned his head and watched as Adam crossed the distance at a half-jog, then proceeded to give each man a thorough inspection for weapons or bugs. Once he gave the all-clear, Jenkins nodded toward the building. "Mind if we get out of the open now, my back's twitching."

Maggie's whole body was screaming warning signals, but there was little she could do about it, especially after all the resolve she'd shown about returning to the field. The hay shuffled and she grimaced. If a mouse ran out, she couldn't be blamed for the consequences. Shifting position so she'd have a better angle on the newcomers, she squinted past the dust motes floating in the shafts of light streaming through the breaks in the roof and waited to see what other surprises might be in store for their little soirée.

The men entered, one at a time, with Amanda standing to the side and Adam taking up the rear. Now that they were closer, Maggie could get a better look at the strangers. The first one into the cavernous space was the Fed. She'd known he was tall, but now, with Adam as a guide, she would place him to be six-four at least, with wide, brawny shoulders, a broad chest, and narrow hips leading down to long muscular legs. This was *not* the type of guy to turn your back on. The other man seemed almost effeminate in comparison, but of the two, he was the one that worried her the most. He was skittish and plainly not happy to be part of this little meet-and-greet situation. She could relate.

"Introducing me to your friends?" Jenkins asked, green eyes constantly scanning the area.

"Not important, they're with me. Let's get down to business. What does Finch bring to the table?"

Brian stiffened at the mention of his name and scowled at Jenkins. "*He's* trying to get me killed, that's all I know."

Jenkins' grin was a slash of white against his tanned skin. "C'mon, Finch. If you're not living on the edge, you're taking up space, right?"

"Whatever, man. I just want this over with so I can get on with my life—hopefully without you jerks in it."

"I'm not feeling the love, brother." Jenkins gave the other guy a pop to the shoulder that knocked him off balance, before focusing on Amanda. "Shipment's a go for this weekend. Give them the deets, *partner*."

Finch rubbed his arm and stared at his feet. "Freight is brought in with cattle trailers. They come through the border late at night and make sure their papers are in order, but, even then, some trucks are stopped. X-ray imaging can spot almost anything from hidden panels under the floor to fake walls, but Rivero is too smart for that. He has connections in Nicaragua. They load plastic covered parcels into the intestines of cows. Each one can carry up to a hundred and thirty-two pounds of cocaine. They're given water, no food, for the trip and the drugs are virtually undetectable." He glanced up, sporting a fat lip and hair in his eyes. "To make it look legit, Rivero arranges sales for the cattle to reputable dealers up north, except he can't sell *those* cows, of course, so he off-loads them in a designated area, helps himself to the local livestock, and carries on down the road, no one any the wiser."

"And you know where this designated area is, I assume?" Amanda stared at him skeptically.

Brian frowned. "Look, I don't need this shit. I told you this was a bad idea," he snapped at Jenkins.

"Calm down, you're overreacting." Jenkins didn't have to

say, '*again*', it was obvious from the disgusted look he leveled on his stoolie. "Like it or not, if you want to ever have a chance of escaping the life, you gotta give us what we need."

Adam shook his head. "I've seen his kind before. He's unreliable. What if he plays both sides against the middle and gets us all killed?"

Maggie had been thinking the same thing until she saw the wounded look on Finch's face. Rising, she holstered her gun and walked toward him, ignoring Adam's hiss to stay away. "I've been where you are," she told him, only viscerally aware of the people around them. "I was used by someone bad, as well. The *only* way to get past it, Brian, is to fight back. Can you do that?"

Finch stared at her and something about her expression must have rung true because he slowly nodded. "I'm ready."

25

Jessica and Chris had been trekking for what felt like forever, though when she glanced at the tech-watch Nick had bought for her birthday, only five hours had gone by. At first, the thrill of a new adventure had kept her steps light and spirits high. But, as the sky became leaden with menacing dark clouds and the trees loomed tall and intimidating the further along the forested trail they traversed, the more she second-guessed her decision to go camping. The warmth and comfort of home beckoned louder and louder with every step she took away from town.

"How much longer?" Chris asked, his voice muted as he lagged behind.

Jess stopped near a fork in the path, a fallen tree covered in moss providing a natural resting place. She sat and took a long pull from her water bottle while Chris hobbled to join her, his lips pressed into a thin line.

"What's wrong?" Jess used her bottle to point at the foot he was obviously favoring.

He shrugged and slung the heavy pack off his shoulders, letting it fall to the dirt with little regard as to what he might be squashing. "Just a blister, my shoes are too loose." They had to leave the bikes behind when his tire went flat and neither one knew how to repair the tube.

Sighing, he pulled out his water bottle and took a small sip before returning it to its pouch on the side of the bag. "Better watch how much you drink, if we don't make camp tonight there won't be any for the hike tomorrow."

Shoot, he was right. She'd been so thirsty she hadn't thought ahead, some team leader she was turning out to be. This deep into the woods, what little light was left—after being chased away by the clouds—was fast disappearing. Instead of stumbling around in the dark, they might be better off building their tent right here. At least they'd be protected from the brunt of the storm rather than being caught out in the open campsite.

"I think we should stay here for tonight. That way you can care for your heel and we can setup before dark." She glanced up as rain sprinkled on her head. "And get out of the rain."

Chris nodded, his shoulders slumping with relief.

"Works for me. That way if..." He stopped, his cheeks flushing.

"What?" She asked, then gasped. "You're hoping Nick comes looking for us, aren't you?"

"*Aren't you?*" he countered, his chin in the air. He waved his arms around them. "We don't need to get lost in the back of beyond to prove some point to your dumb want-to-be boyfriend. C'mon, Jess. If he doesn't like you for who you are, he doesn't deserve you."

Stunned, she took in Chris's belligerent attitude and frowned. "I thought you were my best friend."

He rolled his eyes and turned away to dig out the battery-operated lamp they'd brought along for night-time use. "I *am* your friend, silly. That's why I can say stuff like that, and you're supposed to listen—that's how it works with true friends."

He continued to quietly set up their camp for the evening, untying the tent from the bottom of his pack and pulling out the lightweight sleeping bag rolled into a tight ball. As the rain began to fall in earnest, Jess dove into her bag for the bright yellow rain jackets she'd packed at the last minute, sparing Jake an apologetic glance as he huddled under a nearby tree watching them.

"Here," she said, shaking one out for Chris to wear. He smiled as he accepted the coat, and she was struck by how mature he seemed. He'd always been thoughtful and considerate, but now it was layered with authority, the child turning into a young—and attractive—man.

Confused by her wandering thoughts, she grasped the handle of the lamp and rose. "I'm just going to, you know—be right back."

Chris nodded, though his brows lowered. "Don't go too far, okay?"

Sensible advice, but she needed privacy to answer the call of nature. She whistled for Jake to follow and walked up the right fork of the trail until she crested the hill and started down the other side. Glancing back, she shivered. The path, cloaked in mist and shadows, reminded her of that dinosaur movie Chris loved so much.

Wading through thigh-high ferns, she carefully stepped off the trail, the lantern held high to shed light as far as she could get it to go. "Far enough," she muttered, and set the lamp on the ground to do her business. "Hurry, hurry, hurry," she chanted, seriously creeped out now. Flying insects dive-bombed the light, their buzz adding an eerie addition to the choir of rustling leaves, creaking branches, and the drip, drip of rain on her hood. That's it, she wasn't going to eat or drink another thing until she got home.

She zipped her pants and bent to pick up the lantern, then froze. Something was nearby. The woods had taken on a stillness, as though holding its breath. And maybe it was her imagination, but it felt like someone, or some *thing*, was staring at her—waiting.

Jess screamed.

***

Nick and Jared had been driving for hours. They'd started out the moment the plane taxied down the Sea-Tac runway and hadn't stopped for more than a drive-through coffee and a piss—and still no kids.

Jared had his cell phone out and was stabbing at the keys. "The chief will be here in the morning, he couldn't get an earlier flight."

At any other time, Nick would be thrilled to have Frank in town, but not this way. The guilt and fear were tearing him apart. "Jared, I'm sorry, man. I can't believe this is happening again. It's like a bad version of The Twilight Zone."

The terror of having their children kidnapped by Sergei Barnikov sat like a lead weight between them. Jared straightened in his seat and rolled down the window, allowing fresh rain-washed air to flow into the car.

"It smells better here," he said. "I had cow dung seeping into my pores."

Nick gave a startled laugh. "That good, huh?"

"Worse." Jared smirked and the tension escaped out the window. "I can see why Frank loves it out there. Wide open spaces, room to breathe, and a view that goes on forever, but it's not for me. I like my conveniences. I don't want to drive for two hours to grab a carton of milk."

Nick snorted. "What do you think those cows are for?" He was glad his friend wasn't thinking of moving south. He and Annie had built a good life in Tidal Falls. Jared's mom loved having her grandkids nearby, and now that she was semi-retired from the café, she often took his and Jared's kids for a night on the weekend so they could *date* their wives.

The drizzle turned into a steady rain, making it next to impossible to see into the gloomy forest lining the road. He turned his wipers to a steady swish and the headlights on high beam, but it didn't make a difference. When he caught up to Jessica... she would get the biggest hug of her life—and then he'd ground her until she was twenty.

"Any word on the home front?" he asked, reaching to turn up the defrost. It was cooling down as night fell. They were smart kids; he had to believe they were prepared for the elements, but that didn't stop his gut from churning.

"Nothing so far. The sheriff is going door-to-door. Annie is trying to hold it together for the baby, but she's scared. Hell, so am I," Jared admitted, his voice gruff.

Nick grimaced and tightened his grip on the steering wheel. Both he and Jared had come into fatherhood about the same time; he'd fallen in love with Sara and her daughter, and Jared had returned from duty to find out he had a son. It made the gift of their children that much more precious.

"*Hooyah,*" he murmured, in full agreement. He'd face

insurgents any day of the week before he went through anything happening to his kids. *Not* that anything *had* happened. They were no doubt on their way home, wetter, colder, and, hopefully, wiser. The two convicts roaming around the countryside were absolutely nowhere in their vicinity—he prayed. Thank God, Jake was with them.

"There's something I need to tell you," he started, not sure how to break the news to his friend.

Jared turned his way. "If it's bad news, I don't want to hear it."

And I don't want to tell it. Nick swallowed around the ball in his throat. "We could have a problem then," he admitted.

"Spit it out," Jared growled, winding the window partway.

"There might be more—" A scream from far off on their right cut off his confession midstream. Nick slammed on his brakes and had his door open before the car quit moving. "That's Jessica," he cried, rounding the car and speeding across the road.

His feet slid out from under him in the slippery ditch, but he managed to regain his footing before he went down. His heart battered his chest, all kinds of horrifying scenarios running through his head. If only he hadn't backed out of taking them on the trip, this never would have happened. It didn't matter anymore that he'd done it for their safety—this was his fault and he'd have to live with it if anything happened to her or Chris.

Jared was a near-silent shadow on his six, the two of them instinctively reverting to their SEAL training. As he moved through the undergrowth, he kept an eye out for something to use as a weapon. The forest floor was filled with landmines in the form of broken branches and brittle leaves. It slowed him down more than he wanted, but he couldn't take a chance on announcing his arrival in case the kids weren't alone.

A light flickered ahead through the trees and he glanced over his shoulder to see if Jared had noticed. One quick nod and a couple of hand signals later, they split apart, Jared going wide to come up behind whatever it was they were about to face.

Nick wasn't a religious man, but he prayed now to whatever god would listen. *Please, please let the kids be safe.* Keeping a low profile, he slipped from one tree to the next, slowing when he heard the murmur of voices. Chris. He was sure of it. Much as every fiber of his being told him to, charging in blind was foolhardy, so he forced himself to wait for Jared's signal.

At least now he had a partial view of the trail the kids must have been taking and knew a moment of pride that Jess had gotten them this far. She was smart and resilient, the child of his heart. The light turned out to be the battery-operated lantern he'd bought for their ill-fated tenting trip.

Obviously, she and Chris had decided to make the excursion a reality. He would definitely be having a conversation about responsibility when—*not if*—they got out of this.

An owl hooted, and when it was repeated twice in succession, he replied with the call of a crow. Time to step into action.

Picking up the rock he'd tripped on earlier, Nick hurled it through the trees toward the lamp. It bounced against a thick trunk and rolled onto the path.

Jessica screamed at the same time as Jake erupted into frenzied barking, and his adrenaline drove him into the open. He had to know if she was injured.

At the same time, Jared appeared from the other side of the trail, menacing with dirty lines streaking his face like war paint.

"Dad," Chris cried, hurling himself toward his father. Jared froze for an instant, his gaze sweeping the area, before dropping to his knees and opening his arms to his son.

"Nick," Jess sobbed, her cheeks pale in the wavering light. She stood there in her yellow rain jacket, trembling and uncertain with Jake standing guard as he broke cover and took a rapid-fire assessment of the situation. No convicts, that he could see, and thank God for that.

He hurried forward, anxious now the danger was passed. "Are you hurt? What were you thinking, Jessica? You scared your mother and me half out of our minds."

Tears blended with the rain cascading down her cheeks,

her expression so woebegone all he could do was wrap her in his arms and hang on for dear life. "When we heard your scream... let's just say I never want to go through that again."

"I... I'm sorry, Dad. I'm an idiot." She sobbed into his chest. "I saw something in the trees and panicked. It... it was a deer." She looked up at him, laughing and crying at the same time. Nick cupped her face and stared across the intervening distance at a shaken Jared. Being a father wasn't easy, but the rewards, when they came, were priceless.

"C'mon, let's go home."

26

F rank was almost to Austin when Nick called. Switching to the slow lane, he clicked the Bluetooth connection on his steering wheel. "I'll be on the nine o'clock flight and should be there before noon. Any word yet?" He held his breath, hoping the kids had made it through the night.

"That's why I'm calling—we found them." Nick's voice was tired but jubilant. "They're fine, Chief, both of them. Our little adventurers thought they could brave the woods and go camping on their own. Gave us a few new gray hairs, let me tell ya." He chuckled.

Frank glanced at the roof of his truck and mouthed a silent thanks to his Abuela for watching over them. "Sounds as though they have a future in the military," he said, signaling for the off-ramp.

"Hell, no," Nick growled. "Pardon me, sir, but I'm fine without passing that particular passion on."

"No pardons necessary, and it's Frank, remember. I'm a civilian these days, just like you." *And who would have seen that one coming?*

Leaving the off-ramp and the heavy morning traffic behind, he pulled into a truck stop and killed the engine. "What about the two convicts you were chasing?" Bad enough the children had disappeared but add in a couple of desperate men and it could have gone a much different way. He took off his sunglasses and rubbed tired eyes.

A semi with a truckload of cattle pulled in, rattling over the speedbumps, the air brakes hissing as the freightliner ground to a halt. Two men hopped down from the rig, stretched their backs, and sauntered into the restaurant, leaving the animals to bake on the tarmac. Frank shook his head, disgusted, and refocused on Nick.

"... was going door-to-door and received a call on a stolen Honda. Seems two men fitting the convicts' descriptions were seen breaking into the vehicle, but before the neighbor —a senior in his seventies—could call the police, they'd jacked the car and were long gone. The sheriff's department put out an APB stating the subjects could be armed and are dangerous, but he thinks they'll ditch the car in the next urban area and hitch a lift with whoever they have working with them."

Made sense. Why leave yourself open to suspicion when a simple drop and go would give them anonymity? Frank tapped his fingers on the steering wheel, considering what he would do in their situation. He stared at the busy truck stop and it came to him.

"Truckers," he murmured.

"What's that?" Nick asked, laughter and a child's squealing in the background bringing a smile to Frank's lips.

"Sounds like free ride day at Disneyland in your house." He chuckled.

"Little Caleb is definitely happy to have his big sister home," Nick confirmed. "What about truckers?"

"They travel hundreds, if not thousands, of miles without getting bugged by the feds. If I was a criminal in need of a safe set of wheels..."

"You'd highjack a big rig," Nick crowed, admiration ringing in his voice. "That narrows the search pool down significantly. There can't be that many semis on the road in the timeframe we're looking at. Thanks, Chief. I'll pass your thoughts on to the sheriff and keep you informed. Are you still coming for a visit? Sara would love to see you."

"Raincheck? I have some things to handle on the ranch, first. Tell Sara I'll be there in time for your anniversary shindig, promise." The two men from the cattle truck exited the café, lunch bags and takeout coffee cups in hand. "Gotta go, buddy. Give that girl of yours a hug for me."

"Will do. Call if you need a hand down there. I'll be on the next flight, no questions asked."

Frank nodded, his throat thick. "Will do. Thanks, man." He ended the call, his chest full of gratitude. He might be retired from the military, but his brothers-at-arms still had his back.

Grabbing his keys, he hurried across the large, paved lot to intercept the truckers. "Excuse me," he called, lifting a hand to catch their attention.

The heavier set of the two, the driver, hesitated and glanced nervously at his swamper. "You talking to us?"

Considering they were the only ones nearby, that was a good assumption. The nerves between his shoulder blades twitched, putting Frank on high alert. He took in the out-of-state plates, the muddy tires and lowing cattle.

"Looks as though you boys have been on the road a while," he stated, going for friendly cowboy.

"Who's asking?" the lanky helper asked, his tone suspicious and forehead crinkled like he smelled something rotten —though that could be the stench coming out of the cattle hauler.

"Frank Stein." Frank held out his hand, then slowly drew it back when his gesture was ignored. "I was just wondering where you picked up your load. I'm contemplating moving some cattle soon and need a good transport company."

The driver gazed at him skeptically. "So, you search the

truck stops? Seems like a roundabout way to go about things."

No arguing with the truth. Frank gave them an *aw, shucks* grin. "Busted. Truthfully, I'm looking to increase my stock without spending a bloody fortune. You two seem like smart men who might be willing to make a deal. What do you say?" He needed to get a look at those cows. If his brand was on any of them, he'd have what he needed to bring down the cattle rustlers.

The driver traded gazes with the other man, then seemed to reach a decision. "S'ppose we could lose a few head in transit. C'mon back and have a gander, and we'll talk money —cash money." He grinned, revealing brown teeth.

Frank nodded. "Of course. What about the paperwork?"

"Don't you worry none about that. Where these cows are going, no one pays much attention to papers, if you get my drift?"

In other words, these animals were on the way to a less-than-ethical meat plant somewhere. It explained how the thieves managed to keep the cattle from being tracked by their brands.

He followed the driver's bow-legged gait alongside the vented trailer. Going by the distressed lowing, these cows had gone without food for a while. "Where did you say you were traveling from?"

"I didn't," the cantankerous old fart said. He reached up

to unlock the hinged doors on the trailer just as Frank caught movement in his peripheral vision.

Senses jangling, he started to wheel around when what felt like a sledgehammer hit him square in the back and glanced off his head. His legs crumpled, his vision exploding into bright white stars that faded to black as he hit the pavement.

27

The rhythmic beeping of medical equipment keeping watch over Frank's vitals woke Maggie from an uneasy sleep. She stared at the steady drip-drip from an IV tube attached to the back of his hand that fed him much-needed nutrients to stabilize his electrolytes and provide pain relief.

Emily slept in the uncomfortable sea-green lounger, a thin hospital blanket around her shoulders. The scare of the last few hours had taken its toll, leaving her face withered and drawn under the dimmed lighting. The window behind her head framed a midnight blue sky dotted with stars—angels of Heaven her momma called them. Maggie was unbearably grateful Frank hadn't taken his place among those stars tonight.

She had positioned a chair next to the bed, so they could remain close in case... She eased her hand under his, finding comfort in the warm weight. They'd been assured by the kindly physician on duty there wasn't pressure on the nerve root attached to the spinal column; his reflexes had tested positive, but there could be neurological complications from the blow to the head. He'd warned them Frank could experience some memory loss from nerve damage to the brain. They would need to carefully monitor him for symptoms related to a brain bleed or broken blood vessels.

All of it meant a slow recovery, something she had a feeling would go against the grain for this man who meant so much to so many. To *her*.

The snowy white bandage circling his head made him seem vulnerable, a stark contrast to the strength and authority he normally exuded, and his skin had a gray cast that worried her. It reminded her of Olga just before death had come calling and her friend had slipped away. She wasn't ready to say goodbye to another person she cared about—he had to fight.

"You hear me, big guy?" She rolled her hand beneath his and gently meshed their fingers together until their palms rested heartbeat to heartbeat. "We need you to hurry up and get better. Who else is going to boss us around, huh?" Tears crested and rolled down her cheeks. "You brought me back to life, Frank. Don't leave me here alone."

His fingers twitched and she froze, not daring to breathe in case she missed the slightest movement. Lifting her head, she gazed in wonder as his eyelids flickered and eased open on a grimace. His hand tightened, then went lax. He stared up at the ceiling, his brow below the bandage furrowed.

"Wha—"

"It's okay, Frank. You're in the hospital." She hurried to stand so he could see her. Wiping the tears away, Maggie grinned at him, her lips wobbly. "You gave us quite the scare."

"Is he...?" Emily hurried to the opposite side of the bed, her clothing wrinkled, and hair flattened at the back. Her fingers trembled as she laid them on her son's chest. "Thank God," she sighed.

"Mom?" he whispered, licking his lips. "What are you doing here?"

The words came out a bit garbled, but Maggie was relieved he seemed to know who they were. She poured water into the blue cup on the bedside table and added a straw while Emily lifted the head of the bed a few degrees. "Here, this will help."

He took a small sip and choked before getting the liquid down. "I can't remember why...?"

Maggie looked at Emily for guidance, but she gave a watery smile, bent and kissed Frank's cheek, then backed toward the door. "I'm going to find the doctor. Don't go anywhere now."

Frank looked at the barrage of machinery he was hooked up to. "No fear of that." He waited until his mom left the room, then turned tired blue-gray eyes on her. "So,

Magdalena. You want to tell me why you're crying at my bedside? If I didn't know better, I'd think you cared."

His lips quirked to show he was teasing but the scare was too fresh in her mind for jokes. "You could have been killed. What were you thinking?" Needing to relieve the stress now that he was conscious, she set the water down and began to pace the room. "A surveillance camera at the truck stop showed every horrifying moment. What would possess you to approach strangers like that without some sort of backup? Are you crazy?" She was working herself into a real snit but couldn't seem to control it. When she'd seen that steel bar come down on his head... She shivered and wheeled around to berate him some more, but he looked so worn out it took the wind out of her sails.

She moved back to the bed and took his hand again, feathering a kiss over the leathery skin. "What were you after, anyway?"

He closed his eyes and she thought he'd gone to sleep, but they opened and gifted her with a warm caress. "Keep kissing me like that and I'll be out of here in no time," he murmured.

A warm blush rose up her neck and coated her cheeks. "You scared me," she admitted, rubbing her thumb across his knuckles.

"I'm sorry about that, but if it made you care for me, I'm glad it happened." He lifted her hand to his lips and returned the kiss, except he turned the heat up about a million watts by licking her palm and then blowing on the sensitized skin, his eyes a liquid mercury.

Maggie's knees turned rubbery and she had to sit, unfortunately freeing her fingers from his grasp in the process. "You're a dangerous man. Frank Stein." She closed her hand around the visceral sensation of the kiss, unwilling to give up the feeling. If he could do that to her with just a kiss, imagine if they made love together. Her body shimmered with heat and a yearning she never thought to feel again.

"I..."

Whatever he'd been about to say was cut off as what seemed like half the hospital staff swarmed the room with Emily bringing up the rear. The doctor in charge of Frank's case entered as the nurses checked his vitals and set up a new IV bag.

"So, you've decided to rejoin us, have you?" he said, as though they were sitting down to tea.

Frank frowned, not impressed with the poking and prodding. "How soon before I can go home, Doc?"

The doctor glanced at Emily, then tapped the chart in his hand with a gold pen. "While I appreciate your willingness to free up a bed, Mr. Stein, in this case you're better off staying with us for a few days, at least. I'd like to run some tests and schedule an MRI, just to be on the safe side. How is your vision?"

Frank's brows lowered. "It's fine. Is that necessary? I

have a ranch to run. I don't have time to be resting on my laurels while you use me as a pin cushion, dammit."

The doctor turned to Emily. "Is he always this charming?"

A young nurse giggled and clapped a hand to her mouth when Frank glowered. "Look, I know my own body. I've been through a hell of a lot worse than this and lived to talk about it. Just sign the release form and I'll be—"

A strident alarm sounded from the heart monitor and the staff snapped into action as Frank's eyes rolled back in his head. His mother cried out his name while Maggie twisted her fingers into pretzels and prayed.

3## 28

A dam frowned at his reflection in the dining room window while listening to a report of *the unwarranted attack of a local rancher* on the radio.

"The victim, a thirty-seven-year-old male, was taken to a hospital in Austin in serious condition, possibly with life-changing injuries. The suspects are on the loose and considered armed and dangerous. If you see these men, or their vehicle, call the emergency hotline immediately."

Half the state fit the descriptions of the perps; it would be like searching for a flea on a dog. For someone to get the drop on the Chief he had to have been distracted, and Adam had a feeling it had to do with the cattle carrier the CCTV picked up. Unfortunately, the two men who'd attacked Frank weren't new to the game. They kept their faces turned away from the cameras and smudged the license plates to make them hard to track. Amanda was in the living room

now, trying to find out what she could from Austin PD while
he was supposed to be calling the hospital. It was just... hell,
he was scared. The Chief had always seemed larger-than-
life. Invincible. It was eye-opening to realize any one of them
could get taken out at any damn time. When he'd been shot
in Iraq, it was Frank and Jared who'd saved his ass. He owed
them everything. If he could find who did this and make
them pay, it would go some way toward alleviating his guilt
over endangering his team that day.

"Any news?" Amanda asked, entering the kitchen and
wandering over to the fridge.

"I haven't called yet. They were just talking about the
assault on the radio. The police are still looking. Did you get
anything?" Her shapely rear jutted out as she bent to get
something out of the crisper, quickening his pulse.

She straightened, holding two navel oranges, and used
her hip to close the door. "Some. Apparently, the police have
their eye on a local smuggling operation, but they haven't
had anything concrete—until now." She grabbed a paring
knife from the butcher block and joined him at the table.
"The semi our guys used has a distinctive ding on the
bumper. It was last spotted turning onto the SH 71 outside
of San Antonio. The decals have changed, but the color is
the same, a dark maroon. Consensus is that they're coming
up from Mexico, unloading contraband along the way.
Sound familiar?"

Shit. Frank had somehow stumbled upon the very men

the feds had under surveillance. Possibly even the same guys who had stolen his cattle.

"What are we going to do about it?" He reached for the knife and took over cutting the fruit into sections while Amanda spread out a couple of napkins to catch the juice.

"Our jobs. We continue on the course we've set out and, hopefully, by the end of the weekend, we'll have the culprits." She touched the back of his hand, sending tingles up his arm. "Don't worry, Adam, nothing will go wrong."

Famous last words. He pushed half the orange slices her way and set down the knife. "I hope you're right. I have a bad feeling about the whole thing, especially after that, whatever it was, yesterday."

Amanda laughed, the sound warm and melodious. "I admit, there were some unexpected moments at the meeting, but we handled it. And now, thanks to Jenkins, we have an inside track as to how the operation works. Without Finch we may not have tied the threads together quite so fast. I consider that a plus, don't you?" She popped an orange segment into her mouth, the juice turning her plump lips moist and glossy.

"Hmm?" he said, staring. His heart panged, informing him he was near a beautiful, desirous woman. Without giving himself time to second-guess his motivations, Adam leaned close and brushed the juice with his thumb, delighting in the cushiony softness of her lips. "I think I have to kiss you," he murmured. Giving her time to pull away and groaning triumphantly when she didn't, he let his mouth take over where his thumb left off.

Sweet.

Tempting.

Addictive.

All that, and more. Adam cupped the side of her neck. The cool silk of her hair skimming his hand shot currents of electricity up his arm. He reveled in the quicksilver fluttering of her pulse, telling him better than words how affected she was by their lightning hot attraction. She moaned low in her throat, the vibration against his lips causing his cock to throb and crowd the zipper of his pants.

"*Amanda*," he chanted, captivated. Sweeping the oranges aside, he grasped her waist and lifted her onto the table, thrilling to her laughing gasp—his personal banquet. Making room between her legs, he nibbled on the tempting flesh peeking above the open buttons of her no-nonsense business shirt.

"We shouldn't," she whispered, even as her fingers dug into his scalp, holding his head against the full perfection of her breasts. Lavender and the unique scent of this woman had him half-drunk with desire. He needed to see what was under the delicate lace tickling his nose more than he needed to breathe.

Leaning back, he slowly, deliberately, undid the remaining buttons, one at a time, his pulse pounding harder with every inch of beautiful, creamy, skin revealed. When, at last, he was done, he took in gossamer pink silk clinging to the lush globes of her breasts while the dusky areolas and hard peaks of her nipples begged for his touch. He could die now and be perfectly happy.

Well, almost.

First, he had to taste the bounty before him. The air was thick with promise. Spicy and erotic. He was beyond grateful they had the house to themselves—even though his buddy was in the hospital. Just for this moment, he was going to let everything go. *Feel*, not think.

His lips closed over her nipple through the silk, eliciting a groan from his throat echoed by Amanda. Her legs stiffened around his ribs, her pelvis lifting, searching. Craving him as much as he yearned for her to sheathe his cock and never let go.

He rose in a rush, his mouth seeking hers while his palm cupped her vagina through the material of her slacks and pressed, keeping rhythm with the rocking of their bodies. Her lips opened on a breathless plea, her eyes dark and lustrous, begging for more. Their tongues teased and twisted, desperate for a closer connection.

Amanda's hands clenched and clasped, cradling him within the vortex of their building passion. She tore at his shirt, digging beneath to get at his chest, abs, the belt of his pants. They were going too fast, but the moment her fingers grazed his cock, he knew there was no going back.

**

Brian gripped the pitchfork and hurled hay between the iron fence rails at his father's cattle, wishing he could ram it between Jenkins' shoulder blades instead. The asshole was going to get him killed. When Rivero found he'd ratted them out to the feds, his ass was grass. He couldn't figure out if Jenkins was playing two ends against the middle or what his endgame was, not that it mattered. He didn't want any part of it, and yet, here he was, squirming like a worm on the end of a hook. Figured really; he'd spent most of his worthless life running from one predator or another. Maybe he should just fall on the pitchfork.

He shuddered and set the tool in the wheelbarrow. If he was going to do himself in, there were less grisly ways to go about it. A rope hanging from the rafters in the barn, so his old man could find him. Though it was doubtful he'd even shed a tear at the suicide of his only son. No, Brian's greatest revenge would be to survive and prosper, and by damn, he was going to do just that.

If he could figure a way out of this mess.

As he neared the barn, a figure detached itself from the wall and ambled toward him—Jenkins.

Stomach roiling, he continued on past the man. "I'm busy."

Jenkins stuck out a foot and tripped him, sending Brian

sprawling over the wheelbarrow. He went down hard, dumping the contents in the dirt.

"What the f…"

"Tsk, tsk, tsk." Jenkins righted the wheelbarrow and offered him a hand up—which he ignored. "Have to be careful. Accidents can happen in the blink of an eye." He nodded toward the house where Lennox leaned against the car snickering, a smoke hanging from his butt-ugly lips.

Brian scrambled to his feet, glaring at Jenkins. "What the hell did you do that for?"

"To teach you a lesson," Jenkins said, bending to pick up his hat and toss it at him. "Number one, when I talk, you listen. And number two, don't turn your back on your enemies—it's a good way to get yourself killed."

Brian scowled. "What do you care? You've already hung me out to dry."

Now it was Jenkins' turn to frown. "Keep your voice down. You trying to get us a matching set of .30 carbine stomach piercings?"

Brian glanced over his shoulder just as Lennox stubbed out his cigarette and tapped his watch before climbing into the passenger side of the vehicle. "Looks like your *buddy* is getting impatient." He turned back to Jenkins. "You planning another little get-together with our new friends?"

"You have a big mouth, you know that, kid?" Jenkins shook his head and rubbed the back of his neck. "Look, Lennox and I have an errand to run. The schedule is getting moved up—again. Rivero is freaking out. A couple of his men broke a pipe over a guy's head a couple of days ago and brought the cops out of the woodwork all over the damn state. We're going to have to think on our feet, and I need your head in the game—got it?"

The only thing Brian *got* was that he was damn tired of being pushed around. He knew things; things that could earn him a free pass out of this life, give him a fresh start in another country with a new name. All he needed to do was to decide who would pay him the most for the information he had to share. *See?* He had his game on, just fine.

"I know who the guy is they hit. It was all over the news last night. Name's Stein. His ranch butts up against ours on the southern border. The county's right tore up about it, the Steins are practically royalty in these... hey, what's wrong with you? You're pale as a damn ghost." Brian put out a hand to keep Jenkins upright or give him a shove if he started to topple over. "Get over here," he yelled to Lennox. If the guy was about to die, he didn't want him to do it on his doorstep. Lennox could dump him at the hospital or in a ditch, for all he cared.

Jenkins swayed like a tree in the wind, his eyes dazed, and skin beaded with sweat, though it was only sixty degrees. "Wha... what did you say?" he stammered.

So, it was a reaction to the name Stein—interesting. "I said I know who your men hit. After all, you're Rivero's henchman, ain't ya?" He eyed him carefully as he repeated himself. "Name's Stein, Frank Stein. He runs the Bella Vista ranch, largest spread in these parts. Why, Jenkins? Do you know the family?"

Lennox strode up, his gaze inquisitive. "What's the kid yapping about now? What family? Are we having a social gathering here, or are we leaving to do what we're supposed to be doing?" He gave Brian a lecherous look. "What's the matter, Finch? You missing Rivero?"

Brian clenched his fists and took an ineffectual swing at the bastard. "Shut your damn mouth," he hissed, missing the mark and falling to his knees. "You don't know nothing. You're no more'n a stupid pawn in Rivero's organization. He tells you to jump and you say... ugh." He gasped in agony as Lennox's boot connected with his ribs. Rolling in the dirt, he cradled his side and cowered under the continued assault until Jenkins finally pulled Lennox away.

"One of these days that mouth of yours is going to get you into a hole you can't dig yourself out of," Jenkins muttered, picking up his hat and dusting it off while Lennox stomped back to the car. "You gotta learn when to say something and when to keep it to yourself, kid." He set the hat on the handle of the wheelbarrow. "Appreciate you covering for me, I owe you one."

Brian lay in misery in the Texas dirt watching them drive away. "And you're going to pay," he whispered.

29

Frank smiled as gentle fingers stroked his brow. "*Abuela*," he mouthed. She'd used that same soothing method to ease his bumps and bruises as a child and he'd always felt better when she was done. "I've missed you."

"*Mi amor*, you must fight. Your family needs you." Her lyrical voice filled his mind and stretched his heart to overflowing.

"Am I dying?" He'd made peace with his mistakes with his first deployment. Putting his life on the line for his country taught him to appreciate all the good and let go of the bad.

"No, child. It is not your time. There are changes to come, *tu madre* will need you."

"I'm so tired," he whispered.

Her fingers gently brushed the hair off his forehead.

Tears leaked from his closed eyes. "Ooh, Franco, my precious boy. You have always been the anchor for the family. Your *padre* is so proud of you."

His father. He'd tried so hard to emulate the quiet strength of the man who'd been his hero growing up. "Is he…"

"Happy?" she asked, reading his thoughts. "He's content. He misses his precious ranch, and you, of course, but is making do caring for His flock—you know your father."

Frank chuckled, the sound rusty.

"He's awake," Momma cried, her hand trembling as it found his on the side of the bed. "My baby is awake."

"I must go," *Abuela* breathed in his ear. "Your father and I love you, child. Open your eyes now."

His lids responded to her request, flickering under the florescent lighting, though he wasn't ready to let her go. "What about Cameron?" he mumbled, but it was too late, her spirit was gone.

"Lord have mercy," Momma sobbed, kissing his knuckles.

"You had us worried," Maggie said from the end of the bed, her smile tremulous.

"What happened?" he asked, his voice a rough croak.

Maggie exchanged a loaded look with his mother.

"Tell me," he demanded.

"You passed out." Maggie rubbed her palm up and down his leg, her eyes soft. "The doctor thinks it was caused by a buildup of stress. Your blood pressure is high. They're going to keep you in hospital for another day to monitor and see if it goes down."

"It's my fault," Momma said. "I've put too many responsibilities onto your shoulders in the last few years. I'm afraid the ranch is becoming a burden."

Frank turned his hand to grasp hers and squeeze. "This is on me, Mom. I know how to take care of myself, I've been trained to handle stress. I just let it get away on me, that's all. When I get home it'll be different, you'll see. And no, we aren't giving up the ranch." *Not without a fight, anyway.*

She patted his hand and stood, swiping moisture from the corners of her eyes as the doctor knocked and entered the room. "We'll talk about this later."

Or never. He'd do whatever it was the doc asked, as long as it meant he could go home and take care of his family— end of story.

"How are you feeling, Mr. Stein?" the doctor asked, his kind eyes doing an assessment before he glanced over the medical chart. "You look better than the last time I saw you." He smiled.

Frank kept his gaze on the doc, avoiding the sympathy he'd read in Maggie's expression earlier. There was a lot he wanted from her, but pity wasn't high on the list. "A hundred percent. Does that mean you're sending me home?"

The doctor tapped the clipboard with his pen. "I'll make you a deal. Continue to show improvement over the next twenty-four hours and maybe... maybe, you'll be home in time for dinner. But first, you're going to have to do some physio to see how your heart handles it, and we need the results back from the MRI on your head—sound fair?"

Fair, yes. Was he overjoyed about another night in the hospital? Not so much. But since he had to work on lowering his stress levels, Frank took a deep breath, let it ease out his nostrils, and nodded. "Whatever you say, doc. Just get me home."

"Can I have a word with you, Doctor?" Momma smiled reassuringly and followed the surgeon out the door, leaving the giant elephant in the room.

"Are you going to look at me, or continue to count the tiles on the ceiling," Maggie said after a few moments, her tone half humorous, half aggravated.

Frank didn't need to look at her to remember how her beauty stole his breath, but the doctor's prognosis had awakened a few home truths. He wasn't a young man anymore. Hell, he probably had a decade on Maggie. She deserved someone who could match her on all levels, who didn't need to watch his frigging blood pressure while making love or chasing their children around the living room. Much as it killed him to think of her with another man, he had to let the dream of them go.

"Frank?" She'd moved from the end of the bed and now stood with her hand on his chest—right over his defective heart.

He turned his head and met her gaze, keeping his expression as blank as he could make it. "Thanks for coming in and keeping my mom company, but you heard the doctor, I should be out by tomorrow, so you can go now. Matter of fact, with what happened, maybe it would be best if you and your team found rooms in town until you're finished whatever it is you're doing." He lifted her hand and set it gently aside. "You heard the doc, less stress."

He smiled through his teeth at the confused, hurt in her eyes, and watched as she gathered her things.

Stopping, with her hand on the knob, Maggie spoke to the door. "I hope you find whatever it is you're looking for. Take care of yourself, Frank." And then she was gone, his broken heart following her out the door.

***

Maggie pulled into the ranch yard, but she couldn't remember how she'd arrived there. Her mind was a foggy morass of pain and betrayal.

She turned Frank's truck off and sat, staring out the window at the house, but seeing Frank lying in that bed, his eyes resolute as he'd told her to leave. The worst part was she hadn't seen it coming. In the days leading up to the assault, it had seemed as though he enjoyed her company and wanted to see where their relationship might lead them.

And now...

It didn't make sense. In the short time she'd known him, Frank hadn't struck her as cruel. He had to have realized his denouncement of their attraction would hurt. She cared about him—a lot, actually. He was solid, dependable, a man she could trust. *Maybe even love.*

Was that what this aching pain in the region of her heart was saying? Had she fallen for the rancher? The no-nonsense SEAL Chief with a maddening set of moral values?

She rested her forehead on the steering wheel and let tears slide down her cheeks. He was doing what he always did, taking care of others. It showed in the loyalty of his friends, the affection of his family, the determination to provide a safe haven for the people he cared about. It was the reason she was here right now. He'd learned of her capture in Mexico and had found a way to rescue her. Frank was a problem solver. He saw his health issue as a type of affliction he couldn't get rid of, so he was giving her back her freedom.

That dumb, sweet man.

He was going to find out she wasn't a quitter, but it wouldn't hurt to let him stew over his honorable intentions until he came home.

Feeling better, she climbed out of the cab and hurried inside, anxious to update Adam on his friend's condition.

The house was quiet, eerily so. She had gotten used to Emily's chatter and the mouthwatering aroma of her baking, the thrill of Frank's voice nearby, Adam and Amanda's constant bickering—their mish-mashed family.

When a quick search of the kitchen and the nearby den came up empty, she decided they must have gone for a walk. Heading down the hall for a much-needed shower and change of clothes, she just about ran into a naked Adam coming out of the steamy bathroom.

"Aah," she cried, covering her eyes. "You scared the heck out of me."

"Mags, what are you doing here?" Adam sounded as surprised as she was. "You can uncover your eyes now, I grabbed a towel."

Maggie inched her fingers down her nose until she could verify, he was indeed decent. "Nice fashion choice." A family of ducks paraded across the front of the white bath towel. "You should be careful. You're lucky Emily stayed at the hospital. You could have given her a heart attack waving that thing around like that."

He grinned, his dimples out in full force. "So, you had time to notice my... *thing*, huh?"

Even though her heart belonged to Frank, she was still a heterosexual woman and Adam was a model-worthy male, so... yeah, she'd noticed.

"Get over yourself, O'Connor. Put some clothes on and I'll give you a sit-rep on Frank. Where's Amanda?"

Adam lost his smile and fidgeted with the knot he'd made in the towel. "I'm not sure. I thought we were... you know, but then she up and disappeared this morning without a word. I tried calling, but she's not picking up her phone—damn woman."

Maggie stared at him. "You and Amanda?"

"Mags. I'm sorry." He reached out, his eyes pleading for understanding, then grabbed for his slipping cover. "It's not you, we've changed. I love you. I'll always love you, but I don't think we can go back to what we were together. Do you hate me?"

Touched, she stepped forward and kissed his cheek. "How could I ever hate you? You're my best friend. My partner. The guy who didn't give up searching even though I broke rank and deserved what happened to me."

He shook his head, water-darkened blond hair leaving wet rivulets down his neck. "No one deserves what that creep did. I won't lie, I was angry, and maybe a little hurt you didn't trust me enough to at least have your back on that mission, but I get it—I do. You've always been a one-woman vigilante. I was just lucky you let me accompany you on most of your crusades. You remind me of Frank that way. Speaking of which, how is the big guy?" He glanced past her, as though he expected Frank to walk down the hall at any second, or maybe it was Amanda he was looking for. Maybe they were both doomed to be unlucky at love. And wasn't that a happy thought?

"The hospital is keeping him overnight for observation. He gave us a bit of a scare but seems to be on the mend now.

So tell me, how long has this little affair with your CO been going on? You do realize it can cause repercussions in the department, right?" She had no wish to be a Debbie-downer but fraternizing with the boss had ended many a career and she would hate to see that happen to Adam.

He frowned and backed away from her. "I don't need your advice on Amanda, thank you not so much. She puts enough roadblocks in our relationship. I've been fighting her on this for months already."

Months? So, they had become close while she was imprisoned. Maybe she should be hurt, but all Maggie could think, was how grateful she was Adam had someone in his life—even if Amanda needed convincing.

"Well, if you hurry up and get dressed, I could have a shower while you make us something to eat—partner." She grinned.

Adam patted his flat stomach. "It's probably safer if I do the cooking, I've seen you in action, remember?" He laughed and ducked into the bathroom before she could land a punch.

Smiling, she continued down the hall toward her bedroom. First thing tomorrow, she planned to—

"Maggie, wait," Adam called, and something in his voice had her wheeling around with dread crowding out the joy in her heart.

Grabbing onto the doorframe for support, she stared down the suddenly gloomy hall at his stricken expression.

"What is it?" He held a cell phone in his hand, his expression dazed. "Adam, what happened."

"It's Amanda. She must have left the message while I was in the shower. Finch, the snitch Jenkins brought to the last meeting, called. He had information and insisted on a face-to-face." He looked up and Maggie's stomach dropped. "She went alone, Mags.

30

Nick cuddled his sleeping wife, his front to her back, waiting for the kids to wake. It wouldn't be long now. Caleb was an early riser like his dad, while Jessica could sleep all day if left to her own devices —teenagers.

Since her little misadventure, Jess had been the perfect kid, cleaning the house without being asked, helping her mom care for the baby, not whining about the punishment she'd received. If it were up to Nick, he would have released her from her grounding already, but then, he was a pushover for the women in his life.

Lifting his head, he nuzzled the side of Sara's neck and was rewarded with a soft moan and her bum grinding against his morning hard-on. His arm tightened around her waist, bringing their bodies into full alignment.

"Are you awake?" he whispered, his hand moving up to cup the underside of her breast.

She rolled over and looked at him with sleepy, sensual eyes. "I am now," she hummed as his thumb flicked her nipple.

Shifting so that he lay in the crux of her thighs, Nick kissed her soft, sexy mouth before moving lower to devote his attention to her voluptuous breasts.

"You are so beautiful," he murmured, spreading kisses in a chain down her belly. And she was. Having the baby had highlighted the curves of her body. She'd never been sexier in his eyes.

As his mouth moved lower, teasing and tasting, her fingers twisted in his hair, the pleasure-pain turning him inside out.

"Now, Nick," she gasped, her legs crossed over his back. "I need you now."

Flowing up onto his hands, he surged forward, burying himself inside her welcoming warmth in one smooth push. One of them cried out, he wasn't sure which, and then she squeezed, and it was over for him. He plunged in and out like a piston, sweat pooling between his shoulder blades and over his brow. He ached to close his eyes and lose himself in the exquisite sensations, but forced himself to keep them open, to stay with her, waiting, watching, until the moment they went over the edge as one—their souls united.

He held her close in a blissful euphoria until the baby monitor on the bedside table informed them their little monster was awake and hungry. He kissed her forehead and started to pull his arm out from under her head. "Stay here, I'll go."

She gave him a lazy, satisfied smile before rolling out of bed. "It's okay, it's my turn. Love you, you know."

"I know," he said under his breath as she threw on a robe and opened the door to go to the next room. He listened to her soft susurrations as she greeted her child and got him ready to meet the day. "And I thank the Lord every day for bringing you into my life."

Turning his mind to the day ahead, Nick contemplated the information he and Jared had managed to dig up on the missing convicts. Now that they'd left the area, and her window had been repaired, Jenny had taken her dogs and returned to the farm, but it was obvious she didn't feel safe there anymore. She'd even paid a retainer to Case Closed to keep up the search for the missing men.

They'd started by questioning other inmates at the Canadian institution via phone calls and had learned the two had ties to the same right wing group Adam's team were working on in Texas. Now, they just needed to figure out the connection and where their jailbirds might be heading.

He reached for his phone on the table and started to thumb through news links, looking for anything that struck a chord. With an election coming up soon, there were plenty of political gatherings, but this association liked to play it safe, so he didn't think they'd take a chance on getting arrested in a location that would be bound to be teeming with police. No, they would look for the attention-grabbing platforms. Something to create disharmony among the masses.

"What are you doing?" Sara asked, carrying the baby into the room.

He hurried to set two pillows against the headboard and held Caleb until she was settled and ready to feed him. Giving his son a kiss on his downy cheek, he handed him over to his mother, "Here you go, Momma." And watched as she tenderly cradled his head against her bosom.

"So, are you looking for his first car?" she teased, humor turning her eyes ethereal.

"Hmm?" he murmured, lost in the splendor of mother and child.

"The phone, Nick. What were you looking for?" She repeated, her expression indulgent.

He looked at the instrument he'd forgotten he was holding. "Oh. Yeah. I was just searching for a big enough reason for two men to escape prison in Canada and risk capture at the border. What do they want in our country?"

"Well," she said, her finger making swirls in Caleb's baby fine hair, "if I was a criminal and wanted to make a name for myself, I'd go for the grand gesture, blow up a plane, or set a bomb in an office building. Oh, wait, that's been done."

His lips quirked at her sarcasm covering the worry every

US citizen carried like a mantle on their shoulders. "I'm thinking these two are more the instigators than anti-heroes. From what I've been reading about this militia, they are all about creating dissention. They're overall goal is to create a rift—man against man. Then, after the smoke clears, they can rise as the new world order with a supposedly better way of life." He shook his head, disgusted.

"So, you mean they step into rallies and rile up those against the cause?"

"Exactly. A little here, a bit more there. Soon, the entire country is up in arms and ready to fight, even if they don't really know what they're fighting for. It's a herd mentality."

Caleb finished feeding, the nipple popping out of his mouth as he sat up in a swoosh and tried to crawl off the side of the bed.

"Whoa, there little man. Where do you think you're going?" Nick grabbed him and swung him up high before he landed on his head.

"Be careful or he'll get sick on you." Sara chuckled.

Nick laid him on his back and tickled his belly, adoring the innocent sound of his son's laughter. It sickened him to know there were monsters who would seek to quell his liberty to choose the path he wanted to take in life.

"We have to *be* the change," he told his wife. "If our generation can't put an end to the lack of acceptance and understanding that permeates our culture, it will only spread the disease. I want a better world for our children and grandchildren, and their children. A world where they don't need to be afraid to step out the door or state their beliefs.

"It feels as though we're on the cusp of a civil war, and that's just wrong. Have we learned nothing from our predecessors?"

Sara leaned over and gently kissed his lips. "You *are* making a difference, Nick. Don't give up on civilization yet. We may be slow to catch on, but we're resilient." She picked Caleb up and patted his back. "By the way, isn't it a strange coincidence that the men you're searching for hijacked a semi, and the men who attacked Frank drove a semi?"

Nick stared at her. "Holy cow, you, my love, are a genius!"

She gave him a saucy smile in return. "I've been telling you that for years."

31

Frank paced the hall outside his hospital room, conscious of his ass hanging in the wind under the thin robe he'd been given, and his new pal, the IV stand, trundling along at his side. Ever since the doctor cleared him to get out of bed, he'd been making this loop hourly, determined to get the hell out of Dodge.

The rooms were unnervingly silent, other than the beep, beep of machines. He hated hospitals, they made him feel his mortality more than dodging bullets in the jungle.

"There you are, I was wondering where you'd disappeared to." The young nurse who'd been checking his vitals caught up to him near the nurse's station.

She was cute, in an irritating younger sister sort of way. "You've already poked and prodded me to death, what else is there?"

She grinned and fluttered around him like a pretty pink butterfly. "Come on now, it wasn't that bad, was it?"

"You aren't the one getting poked," he grumbled, hanging onto the counter as his back twinged.

Of course, she had to notice his discomfort. "Overdoing things will only lengthen your stay, Mr. Stein. Do you need me to get you a wheelchair?"

"He... heck, no," he protested. "I'm not that old."

She chuckled and took his free arm. "It has nothing to do with age. If you want to go home, you need to take it easy. I'm sure you've heard the adage, *rest is the best medicine*."

"How about, *an apple a day will keep the doctor away*," he retorted, unwillingly grateful for her support as they meandered down the hall toward his room.

"Well, if you promise to slow down, I'll see what I can do about an apple—deal?"

"Deal," he grudgingly agreed as she helped him to the edge of his bed. "Can you dim the lights a bit? They're hard on the eyes."

She peered at his pupils, then went over to the wall panel and lowered the lighting over the headboard. "Is that better?"

He nodded and gave a relieved sigh as she helped him into bed. "I'm not usually a whiner," he said as she tucked him in like a child.

"Oh, I believe you. It's the tough ones who complain the

loudest." She patted his arm and raised the rail. "I added a pain reliever to your drip. You should be feeling better soon. Is there anything else you need?"

Maggie. Except, he'd sent her away. She was probably halfway to Las Vegas by now, glad to see the backside of Texas in the airplane's window.

"Nah, I'm good." He closed his eyes and pretended to sleep until he heard the door close with a soft snick. Reaching into the bedside drawer, he pulled out his cell phone and stared at the picture of Maggie he'd taken the day behind the barn. She'd been watching Desert Dancer, her dark hair a banner in the wind and he'd snapped the photo. The woman shared the same qualities as the animal; high-spirited, beautiful creatures. He'd fallen in love with her that day.

Was he really going to let her leave without a fight? He had a feeling it would be the biggest mistake of his life if he did.

Taking a deep breath, he dialed her number, his heart jackrabbiting in his chest. At least he was off the damn heart monitor or he'd probably be setting the alarms off again. His mom entered the room with two cups in hand just as the call switched over to voice mail.

"This is Maggie Holt, I'm not available right now, but, if you leave a message, I'll get back to you—"

His grip on the phone tightened at the husky lilt of her

voice. "Hi, ah, Maggie, it's me, Frank Stein. Look, I'm an ass, okay. Don't go. Call me so I can explain, please." Disappointed that he'd missed her, and relieved he had some time to get his thoughts in order, he laid the phone aside and looked at his mother. "I suppose you heard that."

She gracefully carried the mugs over, set them on the hospital table, and turned it so he could reach before settling onto the chair next to the bed. "Since I'm not yet deaf, yes, I heard you, son. What did you do to that nice young woman?"

Trust his mother to defend what she saw as the injured party. "I didn't do anything to her. It's complicated, Ma. You wouldn't understand."

She raised a brow—which should have been his first warning—crossed her legs and took her sweet time taking a sip of the lukewarm crap they called coffee, before setting the cup down to reach over and pluck the phone from his side.

"Hey, give that back," he ordered, then softened the demand. "Please."

"Hmmm, seems as though you are doing a lot of grovelling lately. Maybe an attitude adjustment is in order?"

How could he be a grown man and still feel like a naughty boy when his mother took that tone? "Yes, ma'am." He watched as she fiddled with his phone, trying to access Lord knows what.

"Let's start again, shall we? What did you say to Maggie to make her leave here yesterday with tears in her eyes?"

Shit. He hadn't meant to make her cry. He really was an ass. "I thought I was doing the right thing, asking her to leave." He turned his head on the pillow and stared through the sliver in the curtains at the clouds banking on the horizon. "I'm nearly a decade older than she is, Mom. How can I ask someone as vibrant and alive as Magdalena to waste her life caring for a doddering old fool?"

She chuckled. "You're a long way from getting a pension check, son. Give the girl some credit. She cares about you, rather a lot from what I've seen. Shouldn't it be up to her to decide if she can handle your eccentricities?"

He turned back to her and quirked his lips. "That bad, huh?"

"Worse," she agreed, smiling as she handed over his phone. "Try again. I didn't raise a quitter."

Feeling better, he redialed and waited, his pulse thumping in his ears. When the call went to voice mail again, he began to get concerned. "She's not picking up."

"Try the house," his mom suggested. "Maybe she left the phone in another room."

Maybe, but his gut was telling him something was wrong. He pushed the hospital table away, ignoring his mom's admonition when the coffee sloshed, and threw his legs over the side of the bed so he could sit up.

Groaning at the persistent ache between the shoulder

blades, he called the house and set the phone on speaker while he stumbled to the closet for his pants.

"Frank, for goodness sake, you're overreacting. Get back in bed this—"

"Hello?" A male voice answered the line.

"Adam? What's going on? I've been trying to call Maggie—"

"It's Amanda. She's gone off to meet Jenkins and the snitch he brought to the old mill—name's Finch. I think it's a setup, Chief. I've got to find her." The panic in his voice made the hair raise on the back of Frank's neck.

"Calm down, O'Connor," he commanded. "Start from the beginning. Who the hell is Jenkins?"

"FBI, undercover. Look, here's Maggie. I need to get ready." The phone crashed, causing Frank's head to explode.

"Adam. Adam, answer me damn—"

"He's gone, Frank." Maggie came on the line. "I can't explain right now, there's no time to waste."

What in the sweet hell was going on? He threw his shirt on over the hospital clothes and yanked on the drawer, nearly upsetting the side table in his bid to find his keys. "Don't go anywhere. I'm on my way. Where the *fuck* are my keys?" he roared.

"Don't be angry, Frank. I... I took them so I could get home yesterday. We'll be fine. I'll keep you updated. We're trained for this sort of thing, remember?" She hollered something to Adam, then came back on the line, her voice quiet, regretful. "Listen, I want you to know, I had a really good time here—the best actually. You, your family, mean a lot to me. I just wanted you to know that."

The phone went dead, and Frank was left staring at the photo of the woman he loved and might never see again.

32

B rian hid in a carefully constructed hide he'd made amid the trees above the line shack and waited for the pretty DEA agent to appear. He'd warned her Jenkins insisted she come alone if she wanted the information, but he didn't trust her, so he'd decided on this cover until he could be sure they had no unwelcome guests.

Back when he was a kid, he'd often trespassed on Bella Vista land, just to see how the other half lived and had come upon this old cabin in his journeys. It had served him well over the years, giving him a place to disappear when his old man was on the rampage—which was like every other week. The ranch hands kept the place supplied with the basics and maintained the structure, but he'd never run into them out here, though he was careful not to build any fires or otherwise show signs of habitation. When he'd concocted this plan, it seemed like the perfect location.

Brian grinned down at Jenkins' ugly sedan sitting to the side of the cabin. It paid to know his way around a computer. It had been a piece of cake to hack into the email program from the guy Rivero trusted with his communications and reroute the message to Jenkins. He'd put together a convincing dispatch telling them to expect a '*delivery*', code for the drug shipment they'd been sent to intercept. Jenkins and Lennox had trotted out here about twenty minutes ago and went inside the cabin to wait, as instructed. That was the trouble with henchman, they didn't think for themselves, but, in this case, it worked in Brian's favor.

He scratched his arm where a bug had bit him and checked the cheap digital watch on his wrist for the tenth time. Where the *hell* was she?

He'd parked his dad's beat-up truck half a mile away and trekked in early this morning, making sure to stay off the road in case she saw a double set of tracks. He grinned. It was kind of exciting pitting himself against a federal agent. Wonder what Jenkins would think after he had the woman as his hostage. The only one calling the shots then, would be good old Brian—the guy everyone underestimated.

The sound of an engine almost had him clapping his hands with glee. Pulling his hat lower over his ears, he hunkered down and watched as a dark four-door car drove slowly up to the cabin. The agent parked but remained behind the wheel, as though debating the wisdom of driving here on her own.

"Too late, girly. Too late, now." Brian took careful aim with the .308 his dad conveniently kept in the truck. *Bang.* The discharge almost set him on his ass and definitely freaked out the woman, who ducked and threw the car into reverse.

"No, no. None of that now," he whispered, swiftly reloading the chamber and firing at the radiator. Steam rose from under the hood. That, and the blown out front tire, effectively cut off her escape.

Brian could see her peering over the dash, trying to get a bead on where he was hiding, but the sound had reverberated through the trees, distorting where the bullets came from. If there was one thing he'd learned from his old man, it was how to be a successful hunter.

"Time to get this party under way," he murmured, taking careful aim at the windshield—he wanted to scare her, not kill her.

The glass shattered on impact and had the desired results. She opened the driver's side door and slid to the ground, the vehicle providing a barrier between them.

"What do you want?" she yelled, her voice high with fear and adrenaline.

"What the fuck, Finch?" Jenkins bellowed, cracking the cabin door.

"Shut up," Brian screamed, sending a bullet into the wood above his head. "I've taken all the crap I'm going to take from you and Rivero. We're doing things my way now."

Breathing deeply, he tried to rein in his temper and concentrate on the agent. "Hey, Fed, you want proof of drug trafficking? I'm giving you these two tied with a bow. All I want is a new name, a new life. We have a deal?"

"You're an idiot," Lennox called. "Rivero is going to hang you by your nuts for this."

"No, he's not," Brian shouted, incensed. "I already figured it out. If you don't want to spend the rest of your worthless days in a cell being someone's bitch, you'll have to turn state's witness. That'll keep Rivero right where he belongs, the rat bastard."

"I'm afraid he's right, Mr. Finch," the agent yelled, peeking around the back of the car, where she'd moved to get some protection from the men in the cabin. "Without the evidence, at best all we have is a circumstantial case—one that a good lawyer could easily get thrown out of court. We *need* the drugs."

Brian cursed himself for the idiot Lennox had called him. Of course, the cops needed evidence, that was how he'd ended up behind bars in the first place.

"Come down from there and we can talk," the agent added, taking a chance on lifting her head.

Frustrated, Brian fired off another shot into the air that sent everyone scurrying for cover, but his brief high of satisfaction died with the fading sound. What the hell was he going to do now? He could kill them and disappear into the wind, but he'd have a bullseye on his back for the rest of his life—which wouldn't last very long with Rivero after him. He could turn himself in and face the consequences—he shuddered; no, that wasn't an option. The only answer was to get hold of that shipment. It was the key to his freedom.

"Hey, Jenkins, have you heard word on the cargo? Maybe we could cut a deal."

"I'm not feeling much like sharing, Finch, after you pulled this trick. Why should I trust you?" Jenkins hollered.

"I've had enough of this shit," Lennox yelled, shoving the door open and getting off a couple of shots from his revolver before Jenkins knocked him out with a frying pan to the head. The guy dropped like a felled tree, toppling onto the rickety deck just as a flurry of bullets erupted from the hill behind Brian.

"What the...?" He tried to turn, but the rifle caught on his hide. He yanked it free, then cried out as the whole thing collapsed, burying him under the heavy weight of leaves and dead branches.

***

Frank drove as though the hounds of hell chased him down the interstate. The normally two-hour drive to the ranch would be more like ninety minutes, but even that felt like forever. His stomach plunged every time he thought of Maggie diving headlong into danger. Thank God the feisty nurse, Carol, had heard his angry shouts and come running. She'd turned over the keys to her new Mustang and snuck him out of the hospital under the doctor's watchful eye with his mother staying behind to alleviate the uproar that was sure to occur. They'd wanted to call the police, but until he knew what Maggie was walking in on, he wasn't taking chances with her life.

He was beyond angry with SAC Rhinehold and Adam for going behind his back to meet with known felons in an attempt to round up the drug smugglers. They hadn't said one damn word about their little jaunt to the old mill and he probably would never have learned of it if Adam hadn't blurted it out on the phone.

But he couldn't worry about that right now; his focus was on getting home as fast as possible and protecting the woman he loved. If he'd had more time, he would have stopped by the house to grab his go-bag. Instead, he was going to have to manage with a banged-up head and his wits alone. "The only easy day was yesterday," he murmured, quoting the SEAL motto.

Fifteen minutes later, he left the highway and traveled at speed down the cut across road between his property and Finch's. Finch. He remembered Spence telling him the kid had gotten out of prison and kicked his ass for not following up on the information. If he had...

Didn't matter now, what was done was done. As long as Maggie didn't pay for the consequences of his inaction.

He slowed as he came up on the turn for the line-camp. He'd remembered seeing Brian there a few times in the past but let it go as he wasn't hurting anything. It had jumped out at him the moment Adam mentioned Finch's name. Nestled between two hills, the cabin was basically hidden until you were on it—as a drop zone, it was perfect.

He'd just pulled to the side of the road, deciding to hike in rather than announce himself with the Mustang's loud exhaust, when he heard the sharp report of rifle fire. Abandoning any thoughts of a covert attack, he gunned the engine and roared down the rutted gravel road, his heart pounding harder than the pistons beneath the hood.

Rounding the corner, he slammed on the brakes twenty feet away from the stranger crouched near the back of a shot-up Oldsmobile, a woman's dark head resting near his feet.

Frank's vision tunneled and his hands turned clammy on the steering wheel. "Maggie," he moaned. "Dear God."

Rage flooded his chest, hot and welcoming. He shoved the door open and came out in a rush, crossing the distance between him and the man who'd hurt her. Before the guy could get to his feet, Frank bowled him over and started pummeling; chest, head, arms, whatever he could reach. The red of bloodlust swirled around him, filling his heart and lungs, pushing out the agony of seeing Maggie on the ground.

"Frank, stop," a voice yelled nearby. "It's not what you think." Hands pulled at his shoulders, trying to dislodge him off the enemy's body, but he was deaf to the words—an animal in pain.

It was only because the guy refused to fight back, only

lifting his arms to protect his head, that he eventually rolled off him and lay in the dirt, panting.

"You could have killed him," Rhinehold said. "He's one of ours, Frank."

Frank let his head flop to the side, then sat up, stunned. "You're not Maggie," he croaked. Amanda leaned against the back tire of the car, her Glock in hand as she staunched the flow of blood from her upper arm. "You've been shot."

She smiled lopsidedly. "Pretty observant for a SEAL." She nodded up the slope. "Maggie is fine. She and Adam had some garbage to collect."

Sure enough, they appeared on the hill, a disheveled Finch handcuffed between them. When Maggie noticed him, she broke into a trot, dragging the others behind her. "What are you doing here?" she called. "I told you we could handle it."

Frank grinned, suddenly, incredibly happy. "So you did." He stood and met her halfway. "Hello, my love."

She stumbled to a halt. "Wha... what did you say?"

Adam grinned and slapped his arm on his way by with the prisoner. "You romantic, you."

Ignoring his friend, Frank stepped into her space and tipped her chin before giving her a soft, welcoming kiss. Lifting his head, he gazed into her beautiful eyes and repeated the words he planned to say every day until he died. "I love you."

Maggie's eyes filled with joy and she threw herself into

his arms. "I love you, too." She laid a string of kisses from his chin to his jaw, then leaned back to smile up at him. "Even if you are an ass."

He laughed. "So, you do listen to your messages occasionally." He hugged her close and whispered in her ear. "I really am sorry, I guess I got scared."

She nodded. "From now on, we can be scared together, okay?"

Hoo-yah.

Voices down below reminded him they weren't alone. He kissed her cheek. "You better get down there, Agent Holt. You have a job to finish."

As they neared the car, he could see Adam administering first aid to Amanda, and the back of the stranger as he watched over the felons. While Maggie went to check on her boss, he strolled over to apologize to the guy he'd flipped out on.

"Hey, sorry for the misunderstanding," he said, holding out his hand.

The other man slowly turned, and the ground disappeared beneath Frank's feet. "*Cameron?*"

33

The dinner table was crowded, but laughter and good food made up for the congestion. It didn't hurt that Maggie sat thigh-to-thigh with Frank on the bench, though it made it more difficult to track the conversations. Not that he minded.

He squeezed her hand where he held it under the table, and she shot him a warm, intimate look before returning to the chat she was having with his brother.

Cameron.

He'd dared to dream his brother would rejoin the family one day but hadn't really believed it could come true. His mother was ecstatic, of course. Her baby boy, home again. For his part, it was more complicated. He'd tried to understand and accept Cam's explanation of leaving home in search of himself and ending up in the FBI, but there were a lot of gaps in between. And there was no denying he was hurt. All those years, and no word.

But Lord it was good to have him back.

"What are you thinking?" Maggie whispered, her breath sighing in his ear sending warm tingles down his spine.

"How soon we can make our excuses," he said, knowing it would make her smile. They were gifts, those smiles.

"You like me. You want to spend time with me. You want to kiss me," she softly sang off-key, parodying a verse from the movie she'd made him watch a couple of nights ago.

He grinned and rubbed his thumb along the inside of her thigh. "Hell, ya."

"I don't think I've ever seen you so happy." Adam broke into the private moment from across the food-laden table. "It looks good on you, man." He nodded his approval, then turned to fuss with Amanda's sling. "The right woman can change a guy's life."

Instead of appreciating his touch, Amanda's brows furrowed. She leaned back, pushing his hands away. "I was going to wait, but now is as good a time as any." She looked at Cam, who nodded. "I've talked with my supervisor and we've decided it would be in my best interests to request a transfer as my position has been..." her glance slid off Adam, "compromised."

Adam jerked as though he'd been hit with a cattle prod and Maggie's fingers tightened around Frank's. The table went silent, then Adam burst out with a harsh laugh.

"So, that's it? One night together and you're on the run?" He stared at her sardonically. "I never took you for a chicken, *SAC Rhinehold*."

Frank winced. He could cut the tension between those two with his mom's butter knife. "Adam—"

Amanda waved him off and stood. "Contrary to O'Connor's inflated ego, this has nothing to do with him. Need I remind you we are still in the middle of a time sensitive investigation? It's been decided that Jenkins—Cameron—will take over lead as the priorities have changed. There is now credible intelligence describing a possible threat to CONUS. The DEA will, of course, back up the efforts of the FBI to stop the violent extremists involved before we have a war on our hands."

She gave Emily and Spencer a wobbly smile. "I'm sorry to ruin your homecoming dinner, excuse me."

Frank frowned, absorbing the information she'd shared before leaving the room while Maggie reached over the table for Adam's hand.

"She didn't mean to hurt you," she told him. "Go to her, talk it out."

"And say what?" He gazed at her with pain-filled eyes. "She made herself clear—we're done." He rose. "I need some air. Thanks for dinner, Mrs. S., it was delicious." Head down and back bowed; he strode out the back door.

Maggie turned. "Are you going to help him?"

Frank nodded. As uncomfortable as he was with

personal shit, he knew his buddy needed him. "Give him a few minutes to walk it off. Right now, I want a private chat with my brother."

Maggie leaned up to kiss his cheek. "Stay calm. You don't want to lose him now that he's back."

No, but he definitely deserved some answers. "Hey, Cam, got a minute?"

"Ain't no one gonna eat the meal your momma put out?" Spence glared, a forkful of tender venison steak in hand.

She sighed. "It's okay. You boys have some hashing out to do, but don't forget, we're a family. We forgive and move on —understood?"

"Yes, ma'am," Frank and Cam replied at the same time. Cameron grinned. "You owe me a beer."

It would be the first one he could legally buy his brother, though Frank had sneaked him a couple on his fifteenth birthday—just before Cam disappeared.

He followed the younger man out the door, impressed with the difference the years had made in Cameron's self-confidence as much as his build. As they settled, Cam on the swing, Frank in his favorite spot on the rail, he glanced around but saw no sign of Adam. Maybe his friend had gone to the barn, he seemed to find peace within its walls.

"I remember Ma rocking us boys on this thing. It still creaks the same way." Cameron's teeth flashed in the shadows.

"She won't let me change the chains. One of these days I

expect they'll let go," Frank said, caught up in memories of his mother reading to them while they waited for their father to come home.

"As long as it's not tonight," Cam said, testing their strength. "Look, I know you're disappointed in me..."

"Not disappointed." Frank shook his head. "How could I be? You've turned your life around. Made something of yourself. But, what about us, your family? Mom was a mess after you vanished. Hell, we all were." He stood, frustrated. "Ten years without a phone call to tell us you were even alive. Why, Cameron?"

Cam slowed the swing to a halt and stared out across the land. "This place intimidated me, did you know that?" He carried on without waiting for Frank's reply. "You. Dad. You thrived out here. I felt smothered. Like day-by-day the dirt was seeping into my pores until I couldn't breathe anymore. I had to get out."

He turned to Frank, his eyes shining. "I'm sorry, man. I know I hurt you and Ma, but after Dad died and those rumors erupted at school, I didn't fit in. It was either leave, or let myself wither away."

"Wither away? I *tried* to be there for you. All you needed to do was talk to me or Ma, Cam. You never said a word." Frank had promised he would forgive, as his mother wanted, but none of this made sense.

Cameron gave a harsh laugh. "I know it's hard for you to grasp, big brother, but we aren't all superheroes like you. Us mortals, we make mistakes. That's what I did," he said quietly. "I made one mistake after another until there was no going back."

Frank frowned, hating that from the tone of his voice, his brother had gone through some tough life lessons on his own. "Then what?" he asked, curious as to how he'd managed to turn it all around.

Cam started to swing again, smiling at the creak, creak. "I got caught breaking and entering. Since I wasn't in the system and it was a first offence, the judge let me go, with the provision I do a couple hundred hours of community service for the guy whose house I had tried to rob.

"Turned out he was an Associate Assistant Director in the FBI. I guess he saw something in me, because he basically took me under his wing. Within a few years, I had graduated and joined the ranks as a NAT—a trainee. That's when I discovered undercover work. I've been doing it ever since."

Not so different from Frank's journey into the military, though he hadn't resorted to theft. "I'm proud of you, man, I am. I'm sorry you didn't feel able to reach out to us, but we're here now, and that's what counts."

Cameron rose and strode over to wrap Frank in his arms. "I missed you, bro."

Frank swallowed around the lump in his throat and smacked his brother's back. His mother was right—family forgives and moves on.

PREVIEW MAGGIE'S REVENGE

DEA Special Agent Maggie Holt is fierce, smart, beautiful-- and in over her head.

Undercover DEA Agent, Magdalena Holt, has experienced the seedy underbelly of human trafficking. Sent to capture a drug king she finds more than she bargained for and is held captive for months before she escapes.

Now, Maggie is after one thing, revenge.

Read the exciting continuation of the Wounded Hearts saga today!

The dust and heat beat down on Maggie and the other women in the Humvee. She glanced back the way they'd come. Dangerous as it was, they needed to find a better used road in order to hide their tracks. The goat trail they were on would lead anyone chasing straight to them.

The sun directly overhead made it hard to know which way they traveled. Every bump and rut exacerbated the wound on her side until it felt as though she was getting jabbed by a red-hot poker. She hoped it wasn't festering, but there wasn't much she could do about it out here.

Olga glanced at her from the driver's seat. "You should drive, you'd be much better than me. I don't even have a license."

That's right, Olga was such a commanding presence, Maggie had forgotten she'd been a child prostitute before her capture by the traffickers.

"No, you're doing fine. I need to keep watch." She tapped the rifle, aware of her friend's aversion to firearms.

"What's going to happen to us?" a woman-child asked from the back. Two women huddled on the narrow seat, the body of the young girl who'd given her life for them wrapped in a blanket on the floor at their feet.

Maggie wished she had a positive reply. Truth was, unless they found help soon, they were in as much or more danger than before. This area was overrun with warring factions from two of the most powerful cartels in Mexico. If they were found, they would die.

She forced a smile for the girl. "We're heading for the border and then we're going home to our families and a nice hot bath. Okay?"

The girl looked out the front window at the undulating sea of sand and something heartbreakingly sad passed over her face.

"Sure," she said.

Get your copy today

MY GIFT TO YOU!

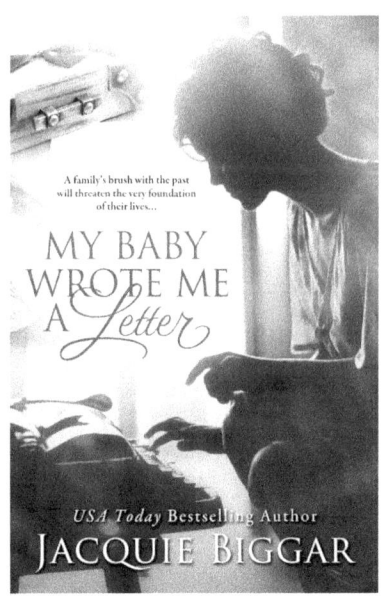

My Baby Wrote Me A Letter

A family's brush with the past will threaten the fabric of their lives.

Eight months pregnant and her Navy husband away on a mission, Grace Freeman craves the security of her childhood home in Canada.

When a letter written by her long-lost mother is found in an old writing desk it creates a tear in the fabric of her family.

Can Grace find a way to bring peace to those she loves, or will a message from the past destroy their future?

Newsletter subscribers also get bonus content and insider information every month. I love giveaways and there is lots of interesting stuff for me to share with you!

Newsletter- Sign up Now!

AFTERWORD

Reviews are the lifeblood of any successful author. Without you, we can't be heard. If you enjoy the story, please consider sharing on your favorite social media sites:

Please click here to post a review:

Amazon

BookBub

Goodreads

Thank you,

Jacquie Biggar

ALSO BY JACQUIE BIGGAR

Wounded Hearts Series

Tidal Falls

The Rebel's Redemption

Twilight's Encore

The Sheriff Meets His Match

Summer Lovin'

Wounded Hearts Box Set

Maggie's Revenge

With This Heart

The SEAL's Temptation

Secrets, Lies & Alibis

Mended Souls Series

The Guardian

The Beast Within

Virtually Gone

Gambling Hearts

Hold 'Em

Crazy Little Thing Called Love

My Girl

Married to The Texan- Box set

Blue Haven

Sweetheart Cove

Sunset Beach

Men of WarHawks

Skating on Thin Ice

The Player

Single Titles

Silver Bells

The Lady Said No

My Baby Wrote Me A Letter

Tempted by Mr. Wrong

Valentine: A Hearts and Kisses Romance

Mistletoe Inn

The Sister Pact

Perfectly Imperfect

ABOUT THE AUTHOR

Jacquie Biggar is a USA Today bestselling author of romance who loves to write about tough, alpha males and strong, contemporary women willing to show their men that true power comes from love. She lives on Vancouver Island with her husband and loves to hear from readers all over the world!

In her own words:

"My name is Jacquie Biggar. When I'm not acting like a total klutz I am a wife, mother of one, grandmother, and a butler to my calico cat.

My guilty pleasure are reality tv shows like Amazing Race and The Voice. I can be found every Monday night in my armchair plastered to the television laughing at Blake and Adam's shenanigans.

I love to hang at the beach with DH (darling hubby) taking pictures or reading romance novels (what else?).

I have a slight Tim Hortons obsession, enjoy gardening, everything pink and talking to my friends."

Subscribe to her Newsletter and follow her on these sites:

Amazon | Website | Facebook | Newsletter

Twitter | Pinterest | GoodReads | Bookbub